HEARTWARMING

Finding Her Family

Syndi Powell

HARLEQUIN® HEARTWARMING™

ISBN-13: 978-1-335-63371-2

Finding Her Family

This edition published by arrangement with Harlequin Books S.A.

For questions and comments about the quality of this book, please contact us at CustomerService@Harlequin.com.

Printed in U.S.A.

Syndi Powell started writing stories when she was young and has made it a lifelong pursuit. She's been reading Harlequin romance novels since she was in her teens and is thrilled to be on the Harlequin team. She loves to connect with readers on Twitter, @syndipowell, or on her Facebook author page, Facebook.com/syndipowellauthor.

Books by Syndi Powell

Harlequin Heartwarming

Healing Hearts
Afraid to Lose Her
The Sweetheart Deal
Two-Part Harmony
Risk of Falling
The Reluctant Bachelor

Visit the Author Profile page at Harlequin.com for more titles.

This book is dedicated to my Groban Girls: Laurie Peplinski, Debbie Greathouse and Angela Chisholm. We've known each other for more than half of our lives and have seen each other through boyfriends, heartbreaks, marriages, kids, divorces and sicknesses. I know that all I need to do is pick up my phone and call if I need something, and you'd be there for me. And also to Lindsay Kosinski, with whom I can spend three hours sharing a meal and it feels like only minutes because there's so much to talk about. These friendships have been such blessings to me. Now when's the next Girls' Night Out???

CHAPTER ONE

ON A HUMID late July day in Detroit, Page Kosinski paused at the intersection and waited for the light to turn so she could cross the street. The coffee shop where she had agreed to meet her ex-husband, Chad, was up ahead. He'd called and said he had something to tell her. Begged her to meet him at their once favorite place. She wondered what he was about to tell her. Did he want to get back together?

She had to admit that she'd thought about it herself every once in a while, but then she reminded herself that she didn't need him to mess with her life or her heart anymore. The thing she really missed was being part of a couple. Her pride would never let her admit it to anyone, especially her best friend, April, but she liked having someone to come home to. She liked waking up with him every morning and going to bed with him every night. She liked knowing she had a standing date on New Year's Eve and Valentine's Day. She reveled in being one half of a group of two. Her marriage to Chad had hardly been the stuff of fairy tales, but at least he had been there. For a while anyway.

The light turned and she hurried to cross the street. She didn't want to seem too anxious, but she was running late as usual. She opened the door to the coffee shop and groaned at the sight of him waiting at a table. With his perfectly coiffed blond hair and chiseled features, Chad didn't have the right to look so handsome, although the scruffy chin was new. He stood and moved the chair opposite his out for her. He kissed her cheek. "You look…different, Page."

She reached up and touched her bald head. She knew exactly how she looked—like someone fighting cancer. She'd beaten it twice, but it had come back a third time in her ovaries. She only had a few months of chemo left, and then she'd find out if it was gone for good. "You look like you always do."

She took a seat, and he left to order their

coffees. He didn't need to ask what she wanted since she always ordered the same thing. She didn't like surprises.

He returned with their drinks, and she put her hands around the mug in order to give them something to do. "How are you, Chad?"

"Good. Really good." He looked her over. "Should I even ask how you're doing?"

"Why would you? You never liked hearing about all the icky details of my cancer when we were married. That was an inconvenience to your precious life." He winced at her sharp tone, and she regretted the words after they were out. They might be true, but he clearly wanted some kind of truce. She swallowed her bitterness by taking a sip of her coffee. "On the phone you said you had some news."

He shifted in his seat and looked out the window before turning to face her. "I wanted to be the first to tell you before you heard it from anyone else."

Oh. She gripped the mug tighter. "Are you getting married to her?" *Her* being the anti-Page: blonde, bubbly and buxom. She couldn't even say her name.

Chad ducked his head. “Nikki and I are getting married next month.”

“So soon? What is she, pregnant?” She smirked at the thought of Chad with kids when he was little more than a child himself. He blushed and was unable to meet her gaze. The bottom fell out of Page’s stomach. She closed her eyes and took a deep breath. “Get out.”

His perfect features hardened into a familiar scowl. “I knew you’d take it wrong.”

“How should I take it? You cheated on me with her while I was going through chemo. You divorced me when I was still sick so that you could move in with her. And now you tell me you’re having a baby?”

“It just happened.”

“I’m a labor-and-delivery nurse, so I know exactly how it happens.” She pursed her lips. The words she wanted to say fought to come out. The emotions that she kept buried deep inside bubbled up, but she kept quiet and took a long sip of her coffee.

He reached across the table to touch her hand, but she snatched it away. “Please be happy for us. You know how much I always wanted to have kids.”

The urge to punch him grew stronger. “Really? The way I remember it I was the one who wanted kids, but you told me we needed to wait. First, until we had more money. Then it was a bigger house. And we waited and waited until I was sick and then it was too late. But you didn’t wait very long for her, did you?” She put a hand to her flat belly. “Get. Out.”

Chad rose from his chair and put a hand on the table near hers. “Page, you don’t want to end up like your mother, do you? Mean? Spiteful?”

Page summoned all the anger inside her and glared at him. He almost tripped over his own feet hurrying away from her. Once he was gone, she put her hands around the still warm mug. She glanced at the other patrons. They looked as if their lives were continuing as normal, while hers had crumbled a little more.

She finished her coffee and left the shop, vowing never to set foot in there again.

THE KID SITTING opposite him had his head down on the table, and his long dark hair covered his face. He hadn’t looked up since

Mateo Lopez had entered the interrogation room of the Detroit Police Department, and Mateo tried to squelch the desire to leave Scotty to deal with the consequences of his actions alone. But he'd been hired by the kid's mother to represent him in front of a judge, who wouldn't likely turn a blind eye to a repeat shoplifter.

Mateo asked a question that he already knew the answer to. "What was it this time, Scotty? What was it that you had to have and didn't care that you'd end up in juvie for? Again?"

Scotty kept his gaze on the table as he shrugged. "Don't matter."

"Really? Because we seem to end up at the police station too often for it to mean nothing." He sat quietly, waiting for the kid to say something, anything. After five minutes, he took out a legal pad and pen. "This is your third strike, so you're looking at a year of lockup."

Scotty raised his panicked eyes to meet Mateo's. "A year?"

"Minimum. The judge isn't going to give you a slap on your wrist since you're a repeat offender." Mateo leaned closer. "Why did you do it?"

"I don't know."

Mateo doubted that. The kid knew more than what he said. "How about I tell you what I know? I know that your group of so-called friends dared you to take the cell phones. That when you got caught, they all ran off with the merchandise and left you to take the blame. Then you told the cops that you were alone and wouldn't give any names. And now they're all free while you're in here and looking at a year in juvie. Those don't sound like very good friends."

The kid's eyes lowered, and he once more concentrated on the table. "You don't know nothing."

"The truth is, I know the law. Which is good for you, since I can try to get a reduced sentence if you'll give me the names of those friends."

"No."

Mateo might have admired the loyalty to friends in different circumstances, but not when his client was staring at the full brunt of the law if he didn't give up those names. "Scotty, I've seen you hanging out with that gang in your neighborhood. I live there, too, so I expect that both the Four Aces and the Spanish Quarters have been trying to recruit you. And today was a tryout."

Scotty frowned. "Like I said. You don't know nothing."

Mateo sighed and rubbed the bridge of his nose. He grew tired of defending kids who knew better but longed to find a place to fit in. The street gangs were an attractive brotherhood to a kid who had an overworked single mother and no male role models aside from the ones he saw in the neighborhood. Didn't seem that long ago that Mateo had been the one on the other side of the table talking to a lawyer. He wanted to give Scotty the chance he'd been given. To find a way out of the endless cycle of poverty and violence.

He stood and left the room without another word. He found Mrs. Rodriguez wringing her hands as she paced the hallway. She rushed over to him. "What did he say?"

Mateo shook his head. "He won't give up the names of the gang members that were there with him. And I can't help him if he's not willing to divulge that information to me or the judge." He put a hand on her shoulder as she started to cry. "He's looking at about a year in juvenile hall."

She grasped his hand in both of hers. "He can't go back to that place. Last time, he had nightmares for a month after getting out. I can't let them put my baby in there again."

"This is his third offense, Mrs. Rodriguez. The judge won't be lenient. Even if Scotty does tell us the names of his friends, he's still going to jail."

He opened the door to the interrogation room and ushered her in. Scotty sprinted into his mother's arms. Mateo shut the door behind him and walked away, feeling tired of seeing the same story play out time and again.

He walked to the end of the hallway and stared out the window and rested his hands on the sill. After a few minutes, he heard a door open, and he turned to find Mrs. Rodriguez wiping her eyes with a tissue. She looked up as he approached. "What's next?"

"We meet with the judge in the morning, and Scotty will stay in lockup here until then."

She nodded and glanced at the door. "Thank you, Mr. Lopez. I know you will do your best for my son."

He feared that his best wouldn't keep Scotty out of jail, though.

Despondent, he left the police station and drove to visit with friends, hoping that he could find some cheer. He parked in front of Dez and Sherri's house and walked up to the front door. His cousin Sherri answered his knock and smiled at him. "Hey, you're just in time for dinner. You must have some kind of sixth sense about these things." She gave him her cheek to kiss then let him pass, shutting the screen door behind him.

"More like you always eat at seven during the week."

"We're eating out on the deck since it's such a nice night."

Mateo followed her through the living room to the kitchen, noticing how her hair was slowly returning after a recent bout of chemotherapy and radiation for breast cancer. She looked well. Last he'd heard she was beating the disease, unlike his mom, who had lost her own battle years ago.

He swallowed at the memory and brightened as he found Sherri's husband, Dez, singing along with the radio as he dressed a green salad. He raised his eyes to Mateo's and grinned. They clasped hands and bumped chests. "What brings you by?"

He shrugged and glanced around the homey kitchen. Wasn't too long ago that Dez had been a bachelor like him. Now his friend had married and adopted a teenager. He looked good in his role as husband and father. Mateo ignored the sharp stirring of jealousy. "It's been a rough day. Was hoping to hang out for a bit with you guys."

"Sure, sure." Dez took a platter of raw meat and then pointed at the bowl of salad. "Come out on the deck while I grill these burgers. And bring that with you."

Mateo retrieved the salad bowl and followed Dez. Out on the paved patio, Dez put the burgers on the steaming grill and took a seat at the table under the neon green umbrella. He pushed out a chair with his foot. "Tell me what's going on that has you so troubled."

Mateo placed the bowl on the table and sighed as he dropped into the chair. "A client. Too young, too full of himself."

"You're not going to ask me to mentor him, too, are you?"

Over the years, Mateo had reached out to male friends like Dez who had come out of impossible situations to make a better life for themselves. Dez had mentored several young men—one was currently thriving in the military and serving in Afghanistan at the moment. Marcus, Dez and Sherri's adopted son, had also avoided a life in a gang and had finished the past year at school on the honor roll.

Mateo replied, "No." And put his head in his hands. "There's too many who need help. I feel like I'm trying to shore up a dam that's already burst. Why do I even try to help them?"

Dez leaned over and put a hand on his shoulder. "You do it because you love it. And you care about them."

"I'm not sure how much longer I can. Disillusionment is my constant companion."

Dez chuckled at his comment and stood

to check on the burgers. "Well, if you leave your law career, you can give poetry a try."

"Funny."

The sliding door opened, and Sherri appeared with two longneck bottles of beer. She handed one to Mateo. "You looked like you might appreciate a drink."

"Thanks."

She turned and handed the other bottle to Dez, then kissed his cheek before returning inside the house.

"You're a lucky man," he said.

"You could be, too." Dez pointed to Mateo with his beer bottle. "And I know just the woman. One of Sherri's friends is interested in you."

Mateo waved off any suggestion of romance. "I'm married to my job, futile as it seems to be."

"She'd be a nice distraction. If nothing else, you could try those poetic words on her."

Sherri returned with a stack of plates and silverware rolled into cloth napkins. She handed them to Mateo, who stood and set the table. As he finished, Marcus stepped outside and his face lit up at Mateo's presence. "Uncle Matty, what's up?" asked Marcus.

The boy gave him a hug and took a seat next to him. "Sherri… I mean, Mom didn't say you were coming to dinner."

"Last-minute invite."

Dez served the burgers and they chatted as they passed dishes around the table, filling their plates. Mateo took a huge bite of salad when Dez asked Sherri, "What's the name of that friend who likes Mateo?"

Sherri punched him in the shoulder. "I told you that in confidence. And it's just an impression I got by some things she's said."

Dez rubbed where her fist had made contact. "I didn't know it was a secret."

Mateo lowered his fork. "You guys, I appreciate that you're thinking of me but I'm not looking to date right now. I've got too much going on."

"When have you ever had time to date?" Sherri scowled at him as she motioned to Marcus to wipe his mouth. "Seems to me, you went straight from studying in school, on to the bar and now you're trying to save every kid on the street. One date wouldn't hurt you."

Her phone buzzed, and she took it from her pocket and glanced at it. “Speaking of which, she’s here to drop something off.” She pointed at Mateo. “Be nice to her.”

Mateo glanced at Dez. “Sherri invited her over?”

“She didn’t say anything to me about it.” Dez stood as Sherri ushered a thin, bald woman out on to the patio. He snapped his fingers. “That’s it. Her name’s Page.”

Page glanced at Mateo and blushed. “I didn’t know you had company, Sherri. I just wanted to drop off that book we talked about at the meeting the other night.” She handed it to his cousin and paused, looking between them. “Well, enjoy your dinner.”

Sherri put her arm around Page’s shoulders. “Don’t rush off. Join us. We have plenty of food.”

“I appreciate the offer, but I haven’t been able to eat much lately.” She gave Sherri a quick hug and left.

Dez pointed in the direction Page had gone. “That’s her. You’d like her, Mateo. She’s funny and smart. And you know that’s a deadly combination for guys like us.”

He remembered dancing with her at a

party a couple of months ago. She'd been standing alone, watching the others, so he'd invited her to dance with him. It had been one song and then they'd parted ways. To be honest, she was just his type of woman. Dez had been right when he said that funny and smart was an irresistible combination. But he couldn't do it. "No offense, but I'm not looking to date someone dying from cancer."

The patio door opened and Page was standing there. Mateo felt like groaning, and he hoped she hadn't heard him, but her expression told him she had. She handed a pair of sunglasses to Sherri. "You forgot these in my car." She turned to Mateo. "And I'm fighting cancer, not dying from it. Goodbye, again."

Sherri winced and then ran after Page, while Dez shook his head. "Not cool, man."

"I didn't know she was right there." He'd come off as a jerk and he knew it. "But I meant what I said. I don't want to get involved with anyone fighting cancer. You know my history."

His mom had died from breast cancer when he was a teenager. He'd watched her fade away day after day. When Sherri had been diagnosed last year, he'd feared the same fate would befall her. Instead, she'd fought and won. He only wished his mother had won her fight, too.

Dez nodded toward the door. "Still, you should apologize to her before she leaves."

He knew it was the right thing to do. He found Sherri and Page talking in the living room. Sherri gave him a smile before she excused herself, touching his arm as she walked past him. He came forward to face the other woman. "Page, I apologize for what I said out there."

"Which part? Where you said you wouldn't date me? Or when you said I was dying?"

He cocked his head to the side and studied her. She looked rail-thin, and the hollows in her cheeks were deep, like those he remembered seeing in his mom's face. But Page's eyes snapped with vitality and anger. She was even cute in her black T-shirt that had a lace edge along the bottom and hot pink nail polish on her toes that peeked out of her black sandals. He looked at her directly. "Both?"

She rolled her eyes. "Goodbye, Mateo."

She turned on her heel and he followed her outside to her car. "Page, wait! I didn't mean to hurt your feelings."

She stared at him, and he felt as if she was trying to read him. "When you look at me, all you see is cancer. But that's just something that I have. You don't really see me, and I wish you would."

She got into her car and drove off. He watched her leave and then returned to the backyard. When he took his seat, Sherri cocked an eyebrow, and he gave her a shrug. "I apologized."

Dez took a swig from his beer bottle and pointed at him with it. "You'd be lucky to date that woman, cancer or not. I speak from experience when I say that loving a woman who has survived the worst, only makes life more precious."

Sherri smiled and put a hand on Dez's forearm. "It makes you appreciate what you have for as long as you can."

Mateo sighed and put his napkin back on his lap. "I'm not interested in anyone right now. That's the truth."

Sherri stared at him for a minute before

reaching out and grabbing his hand. "Okay. We won't push." A smile played around her mouth. "We'll leave that to the aunties."

Mateo groaned in mock horror but then returned her smile with one of his own. Truth was, Page intrigued him. And though she'd left, the memory of her lingered in his mind.

PAGE LOOKED DOWN at the speedometer and eased her foot off the accelerator. She'd been driving at forty miles an hour in a 25-mile-per-hour zone. *Breathe in, breathe out*, she reminded herself, trying to calm her racing heart.

Mateo's words still echoed in her brain. He didn't date someone who was dying. She tried to shake off the disappointment, but what he'd said still stuck. She'd always thought he was hot, after having seen him at Sherri's party last year and then again at April's a couple of months ago. She'd nearly swooned when he'd asked her to dance. Had reveled in the feeling of his strong arms around her, his hand at her waist. Then the song had been over and he'd moved on. But she'd dreamed of that dance ever since.

She pulled up in front of April's house and let her car idle for a moment before shutting it off. She got out, walked up to the front door and entered without knocking. "Okay, I'm here. The party can begin."

April glanced up from the box she'd been packing and squinted. "Have you been crying?"

"What? No. I don't cry." She peered at her reflection in the mirror on the wall behind her. She appeared a little sad maybe, but no tears. "Where do you want me to start?"

"Knowing your organizational skills, I left the kitchen for you." They entered the room together and surveyed the empty boxes waiting to be filled. April sighed. "I can't believe I'm leaving this place. I'm going to miss it."

"You're only moving two blocks over. It isn't the ends of the earth."

April had recently gotten engaged to Zach Harrison and would be marrying her fiancé in less than a month. Her friend picked up a box and took it to the nearest counter. "He wants to keep his dishes because he grew up using them. Fine, we can donate mine. But I want my coffeemaker and mug collection. Other than that, I'm not sure what else to bring with me."

"What did he say?"

"He told me to bring whatever makes me happy." She looked around the kitchen. "But it all makes me happy."

Page pointed at a spoon that had a slightly bent handle. "Even that old thing?"

April clutched the spoon to her chest. "I eat my morning cereal with it. It's my favorite." She chuckled. "Can you believe I'm getting married? Me? Last year at this time I had just finished chemo and was counting down the days to my reconstruction surgery."

Page put her arm around April's shoulders. "You deserve all this happiness and more."

"I am happy with him." Her eyes got a dreamy look, then she sighed. "Have you decided who you're bringing to the wedding?"

Page snorted. If there was anything she hadn't thought about it was a date for the upcoming nuptials. "What's wrong with coming alone? Besides, as maid of honor,

I'll be too busy taking care of you to think about a date."

"What about Mateo?" April waggled her eyebrows. "Have you thought about asking him? I'm sure he'd say yes."

And Page was just as sure he'd refuse. He didn't date someone dying from cancer. Okay, she had to let that go. But like it or not, the words had hit their mark. "He wouldn't be interested."

April crossed her arms over her chest. "I don't know. I saw the way the two of you were dancing at my party."

"Just drop it, okay? Me and Mateo are never going to happen." She opened a cupboard and started to pull out plates.

"But I thought you liked him."

She paused from wrapping a plate in newspaper and considered her friend's words. "I think he's good-looking."

"And that's all there is? You just think he's hot?"

Page put the wrapped plate in a box and leaned against the counter. "No. I think he's smart. He's a great lawyer, according to Sherri. And I like him." She picked up another plate. “But nothing’s going to happen. He doesn’t like me.”

Maybe if she kept repeating that, she’d believe it. And give up the dream of pursuing something with Mateo. She was dying, after all.

CHAPTER TWO

THERE WAS NOTHING like helping bring a baby into the world. Despite the blood and mess and chaos, no moment felt better to Page. She carefully took the newborn from Dr. Angela Achatz and carried her to the new mom, who wept as Page placed the baby on her chest. "Congratulations," she whispered, as the mom turned her head to share the moment with her husband.

She watched as the couple had eyes only for their infant girl and each other. Page banished the bitter thought of never having that moment herself and returned to aiding the doctor with the afterbirth. Ever since she'd heard about Chad and his girlfriend expecting a baby, the elation Page usually felt at each birth had dimmed a little. She had started to feel hollow, rather than filled with the usual happiness she'd experienced before.

Dr. Achatz peered at her. “Are you okay, nurse? You look a little pale.”

Page tried to smile and nodded. “Yep. I’ll take the mother and baby to postnatal. Then I’ll check on the status of the mom’s room.”

“Tiffany can do that.” Dr. Achatz motioned to one of the other nurses, who nodded and walked over to the couple to let them know the next steps. “I was hoping you and I could have a chat.”

Page hated to hear what the OB-GYN doctor would need to talk to her about. She knew Dr. Achatz didn’t like that she’d reduced her working hours, but the chemotherapy left her tired and in a brain fog. She’d spoken to her supervisor, Joann, about her fears that her fatigue and weakness would result in her making a mistake or miss a doctor’s orders. She refused to put her patients in harm’s way when she knew the risks involved for herself. She rearranged the instruments that the doctor had used for the labor on the surgical tray.

Her stalling tactic didn’t work. Dr. Achatz crooked her finger at Page and pointed at the sinks, where she started to remove her gloves and wash her hands. “How are you really feeling, Page?”

She got really bored of hearing that same question from well-meaning friends. And was even more tired of repeating the same answer. “Better than the last few days.”

“When is your next infusion?”

Page counted the days to her next chemo appointment. “Next week. What did you want to talk to me about, Dr. Achatz?” No point in chitchat if the doctor had something important to discuss with her.

Angela removed the surgical cap from her head and shook out her hair. “I have a case coming up that I’d like you to assist with.”

If she had any hair left, her eyebrows would have raised. “Assist?” Nurses may help the doctor in a delivery, but they didn’t assist. Page frowned and tried to figure out what Angela was up to.

The doctor nodded and untied the yellow surgical dress from around her neck and placed the garment in the laundry bag. “I’m going to need a lot more assistance on it than the typical L-and-D nurse. I need someone like you, with more advanced training. You're still interested in pursuing the midwife program at the college?"

Oh. Before cancer had returned for the third time, Page had talked about taking midwife courses and adding to her nursing skills. She'd even toyed with the idea of going back to medical school for her degree once she was in remission, but she hadn't had a chance to look at the application before cancer had shown up once more. "Things being what they are right now, I'm not doing anything but concentrating on getting better."

Angela studied her as if Page was under a microscope. "Has Dr. Frazier mentioned anything about your prognosis?"

Her oncologist had hopes that the particular chemo cocktail she was on would knock the cancer out of her body long-term. But being a three-time loser with the disease didn't make Page believe in fairy tales of remission. "I'm just trying to get through chemo and eventually make it to the five-year mark of being cancer-free."

"But what if you could get to that five years with your midwife certification?" She put a hand on Page's shoulder. "Think about it. You're a wonderful nurse, but someone with your skills could really advance further. My clinic needs more people like you."

Dr. Achatz walked out of the delivery room, leaving Page where she stood. She took a deep breath and glanced at her reflection in the window above the sinks. She couldn't think about anything right now apart from taking care of her body. Improving her skills could wait.

PAGE SAT ON the empty hospital bed and let her legs dangle. "Can you believe she asked me to apply for the program?"

April stopped filling out paperwork and looked up at her. "And why shouldn't you? You'd be a great asset to her and the patients."

"Hey, I don't want to hear that I need to visualize my future after cancer, or that life continues with or without healing." She groaned and laid back on the hospital bed, her arm over her eyes. "I must be crazy for even considering it."

"You're not crazy. You're looking ahead with a glimmer of hope."

She shot upright and April gave her a wide grin and waggled her eyebrows. "You knew I couldn't resist saying something *woo woo*."

"You wouldn't be you if you didn't." Page glanced at her watch. "I've got about twenty minutes left on my break. Want to get something to eat?"

"You're hungry? That's a good sign."

"Don't read too much into it." She slid off the bed and followed April from the trauma room.

The doors to the emergency room opened suddenly and a gurney being pushed by a paramedic—with a girl on it—sped toward them. April dumped her paperwork by the intake nurse and followed the girl into the just vacated trauma room.

Page continued walking to the cafeteria when she heard April call her name. She turned and April waved her back over to the trauma room. "I could really use your help on this one."

"I'm an L-and-D nurse, remember?" But Page followed her inside anyway.

April motioned to the girl. "This is Ruby and she's in labor."

Page froze, taken aback at how young the patient seemed. "Sweetie, how far along are you?"

Ruby groaned as she grasped her rounded belly. "I don't know. Six or seven months? What's happening?"

Either one was too early for the baby. Page glanced at April. "Has her water broken yet? We might be able to stop labor."

April put the stirrups into an upright position and Page helped move Ruby, so that the doctor could get a better look. She pushed the dark, kinky hair off the girl's forehead. "Dr. Sprader is going to examine you to see if the placental sac is still intact. If it is, we can probably get the labor pains to stop. How long have you been having them?"

"Since early this morning, but I thought it was a tummy ache from something I ate." Ruby's face withered. "I didn't think he was coming now."

"The sac is fine," April told them. "You're only dilated to about a three, Ruby, so we can try to reverse this and give the baby more time to grow and develop."

She glanced at Page, who nodded at the

unspoken request and left the room. She retrieved a fetal monitor and returned to the room. “We’re going to get you hooked up to this so we can watch the baby and the contractions.”

April wrote her orders on a small pad and gave it to the other ER nurse, who left to retrieve the meds. She turned back to the girl. “We’re going to give you something to relax your body, which will hopefully stop the labor. Meanwhile…did someone come in with you, Ruby? Your mom or dad?”

Ruby shook her head. “No, it’s just me.”

Page finished hooking up the cords for the fetal monitor and switched it on. The baby’s heartbeat was strong and steady, a good sign. “Who is your OB-GYN?”

“My what?” Ruby moaned again and clutched her belly.

April exchanged a worried look with Page, then focused on the teen. “You haven’t had any prenatal care?”

Ruby laid back on the bed and Page put her hand on the girl’s. “How old are you, sweetie?”

“Nineteen.”

Page would eat April’s stethoscope if the

girl was more than fifteen. She narrowed her eyes. “Try again. How old are you?”

The girl sighed. “Okay, I’m eighteen.”

Page looked over at April, who hid her smile. From one of the drawers, she pulled out an IV kit and held it up for Ruby to see. “I’m going to start an IV on you. That means a long needle. So while I’m doing that, I’ll let you think back on when your birthday really is.”

“Why’s it matter how old I am?” Ruby grunted as Page inserted the needle into her vein. “I take care of myself. That’s what matters.”

“I don’t doubt that, but we need to get your parents’ consent after a certain point if you’re under seventeen.” Page taped the needle into place on top of Ruby’s hand then took the saline bag the other nurse handed her. “This is a life-threatening situation, so we can treat you now. But when you’re stabilized, we’re going to need to get that consent.”

Ruby frowned at Page as she hung the saline bag on to the IV stand next to her. “I consent.”

April's amusement faded. "Do you have any parents?"

Another contraction hit and Ruby doubled over, ending any further questioning. They worked to get the medication injected into the IV so that they could stem labor before it got too far along. Page's beeper went off and she made a face. "I've got to get back upstairs, April. Do you want me to send Dr. Achatz for a consultation?"

"I'll call her if labor progresses. Thanks for your help."

"Nursing never really stops." Page addressed Ruby, "I'll check on you later. After my shift."

"Why?"

So much for trying to be nice. "In case you need someone to talk to. That's why."

The girl waved her off. "I told you. I take care of myself. I don't need anybody."

Page gave a short nod and left the room, but she felt what had just happened would stay with her for the rest of the day.

THE JUDGE ENTERED the courtroom and Mateo stood, tugging on the shoulder of the young man beside him to do the same.

Scotty still refused to name names and the assistant district attorney had refused to make a deal. So here they were, facing a judge.

The Honorable Jeffrey S. Gorges sat, and everyone in the courtroom followed his example. The bailiff called their case, and Judge Gorges opened the file and perused it, even though Mateo knew he'd be prepared already. "Counselors, approach the bench for a moment."

Well, this was something new. Mateo stood and straightened his suit jacket before walking up to the bench along with ADA Pam Everett. Judge Gorges peered down his long nose at them. "I thought a deal was going to be negotiated in this case."

Pam glared at Mateo. "Talk to Mr. Lopez. His client won't divulge the information, so there is no plea bargain, Your Honor."

"I've told my client what he's facing, but he won't talk." Mateo gave a halfhearted shrug. Whether Scotty tried to save his own neck or not, Mateo wouldn't lose any sleep if the kid did time. Whoa. When had he become so cynical? He cleared his throat.

"He wants to go right to sentencing, Your Honor."

Judge Gorges let out a big sigh. "Third strike, counselor. You know what that means."

"Yes, sir, and so does my client." Mateo looked at Scotty, who stared defiantly back at them. "He's willing to plead guilty and face the consequences."

"He's too young to be put in a system that will chew him up and spit him out." More than a hint of resignation tinged Judge Gorges's words. "We'll proceed then."

Pam smirked at Mateo. He tried to ignore the sinking feeling in the pit of his stomach and walked the few feet to the defendants table. He sat next to Scotty and leaned in to the boy. "Last chance to change your mind about what happens next. The judge is willing to listen if you have some names. Otherwise, we go right to sentencing."

Scotty faced the judge. "Whatever. Let's just get this over with."

"Your friends will forget you while you're in prison. You know that, right? Once you're gone, you're no use to them. They also won't remember how you kept quiet." He hoped that the kid would listen to reason and save his own skin, if nothing else.

"But they'll remember if I squeal. No thanks."

The judge glared down at them. "Will the defendant please rise?"

Mateo stood and brought Scotty to his feet.

Judge Gorges, his facial features somber, his hands folded before him, spoke with the authority he'd been given. "Scott Arthur Rodriguez, with respect to the six counts of larceny, how do you plead?"

Scotty stared straight ahead, but didn't say a word. Mateo muttered to him, "It's either guilty or not guilty, kid."

The bravado from before seemed to be fading. Scotty took a deep breath, then another. "Guilty."

"Your Honor."

"Guilty, *Your Honor*."

The kid's voice cracked on the last word, and Mateo felt his anger and disillusionment melt slightly. Scotty hadn't even finished going through puberty, yet he faced incarceration for at least a year. It hadn't been that long ago that Mateo had faced the same pressure of a gang and succumbed to it before getting out. But he had gotten out, while Scotty seemed resigned to a future of courtroom sentences and jail stints.

Judge Gorges closed the file in front of him. "Mr. Rodriguez, you understand that since this is your third conviction and because of your refusal to assist the police that there will be no leniency?"

Scotty nodded until Mateo nudged him. "Yes, Your Honor."

"Then I see no other choice. Scott Arthur Rodriguez, you are to be remanded to the authorities at the Wayne County jail until a bed is open in the Wayne County juvenile delinquent facility for a term no longer than eighteen months."

Mrs. Rodriguez shouted and rose to her feet.

Judge Gorges pounded his gavel. "Order, please." He switched his attention back to Scotty. "You'll be jailed with the adult male population, men who are hardened criminals. Is that what you want, Mr. Rodriguez?"

Gorges couldn't be serious about this.

Scotty had shoplifted, not hurt or killed anyone. It was a minor crime. Mateo said, "Your Honor, the defendant is only thirteen. There must be another location, another option—"

"With overcrowding in the juvenile facilities, this is our only option. So let me ask again, how do you plead, Scotty?"

The kid seemed on the verge of tears. "Guilty."

Judge Gorges stood and motioned for the deputy who stood on the edge of the courtroom. "He's all yours then."

The deputy approached the defendant's table with cuffs in his hands. Scotty turned to Mateo, the panic in his eyes evident. "He's really sending me to the adult jail?"

"He is."

"I didn't think…"

Mateo put a hand on Scotty's shoulder and thrust the kid toward his mother, who wept and clung to her boy.

Eventually the deputy stepped forward to put the cuffs on Scotty's wrists, even though they hung loosely on him. This wasn't fair, but the judge was right. There weren't many options for this to play out.

After Scotty left the courtroom, Mateo tried speaking to Mrs. Rodriguez. “A court officer will contact you with information about his transfer to the jail. You’ll be able to visit him there shortly, and he’s going to need to see you.”

“They’re going to eat him alive.”

Mateo tried to think of something comforting to say, but he had nothing. There wasn’t anything good to say about this entire situation. “I’ll work on getting him transferred to a juvenile facility as quickly as possible.”

She nodded and left the courtroom. The assistant DA gathered her files and walked to the defendants table. “Tough break for the kid.”

Mateo gathered his belongings and placed them in his leather briefcase. “Come over here to gloat?”

“Not at all. If you ever get tired of being on that side of the courtroom, let me know. You’re a terrific lawyer, Mateo, even if you do get stuck with guilty clients.”

“Right.” He didn’t look at her as he brushed past her and out of the courtroom. He didn’t stop until he got to his car. He sat inside for a moment, debating where to go. It was Monday, which meant he needed to put in some hours at the office, preparing for his next client's trial. Another kid caught in the system. He closed his eyes and took a deep breath. He couldn't do this anymore. Couldn't look into a kid's eyes and wonder how someone so young and innocent could do such horrible things.

He started the car and drove to the office, keeping himself on autopilot so he wouldn't have to think, to feel. It was hopeless. All of it.

PAGE PLACED HER dirty scrubs in the bin, took her purse from her locker and punched out. It had been a long day, and her feet ached despite wearing shoes that were made to be comfortable. She slumped onto the nearest bench and debated her options. She felt pretty good, so she supposed that she should do something productive. Her next round of chemo would take the wind out of her sails for a few days, so she could get groceries while she still had an appetite.

Her thoughts turned to Ruby as they had ever since she'd met the girl. Dr. Achatz had been called in to assist with stopping labor, and Page wondered if they had been successful. It wasn't fair that a girl so young should face this alone, but it seemed like Ruby was determined to do just that.

She pushed off the bench and stood for a moment until the locker room stopped spinning. She should know better than to get up so quickly, but there were times she forgot she had cancer. She caught the elevator to the first floor and found herself at the intake counter. "Hey, Janet, is April around?"

The older woman looked up at her and glanced around the bustling room. "She's somewhere in this madness."

"Did they discharge Ruby?"

Janet's jaw tightened. "You know I can't disclose that information."

"C'mon, Jan. We used to be pals when we worked together."

"Until you left us for upstairs." She wagged a finger at her. "I don't think so."

Page admitted her colleague was right, but still, she needed to know if Ruby was okay. She walked toward the trauma area, but she didn't find Ruby. She was able to track down April as she left a curtained area. "Your shift over already?"

Page shook off the question. "Where's Ruby? The girl who came in earlier?"

April gave orders to a nurse, then turned back to Page. "Why are you asking?"

"Because she's been on my mind all afternoon for some reason. I want to make sure she's okay."

April gave a nod. "She was sent upstairs about an hour ago. Dr. Achatz is keeping her overnight just to be safe." She leaned in close. "I don't think the girl has anywhere else to go, to be honest. And at least while she's here, we can monitor her and take care of her and the baby."

"Good." Page should have felt relief, but the knowledge left her antsy. "I guess I'll go home." The way April watched her made her even more anxious. "What?"

"You should go see her. She was asking about you."

Really? That didn't seem possible, since the girl had made it obvious that she wasn't interested in anything Page had to offer. "What can I do?"

"Talk to her. Maybe get some information that can help her." April gave a shrug. "Maybe you could reach her where we couldn't."

"I don't see how."

"Try." April turned away when another doctor called her name.

After several stops and peeks into patient rooms, she found Ruby sitting up in bed watching a reality court show in the maternity wing. "Hey, Ruby. How are you feeling?"

The girl turned and peered at her. "What are you doing here?"

"I got off work and thought I'd check in on you." Page entered the room and took a seat, placing her purse in her lap. "So they were able to stop labor for now."

"Yeah." Ruby picked up the remote and started to flip through the channels.

Page would need to do more to get the girl to open up. "Are you sure there's no one we can call for you?" When Ruby didn't answer, Page stood and walked closer to the bed. "Where's your mom?"

Ruby paused on a channel. "Dead."

Oh. "And your dad?"

"Don't know. My mom told me his name

and that he was from Detroit, but I've never met him."

Page watched as the girl scanned more channels, although she didn't seem interested in any one in particular. "There's gotta be someone who's worried about you."

Ruby turned her attention away from the TV screen and glared at Page. "There's no one who looks out for me but me. Got it?"

Page sure did. She had been about Ruby's age when she realized her parents were more concerned with themselves than they were about their only daughter. They may have been living in the same house, but neglect was neglect. She'd been ignored unless it was convenient for them to use her in their continual war against each other. She'd learned to take care of herself because no one else was going to.

"Did you run away?"

Ruby laughed, but the sound was anything but cheerful. "You gotta have a home to run from." She returned to flipping through the channels. "Are you done with the questions?"

"Nope." She took a step closer. "Where

are you going to go when they release you from here?"

"Why do you care?"

Page gave a one-shoulder shrug. "Because maybe everyone needs someone who worries about them."

"I don't need you."

"Well, it seems I'm the best you've got right now."

Ruby turned off the television and placed the remote on the bedside table. "You serious?"

The strange thing was Page had never been more serious. The idea of taking care of this girl had been planted hours before, as she'd mulled over Ruby's circumstances, and it had taken root, watered by her worry and concern. This girl claimed to have no family, and the thought of offering her a home had bloomed. Maybe it was because she wished someone had helped her when she was Ruby's age. That an adult might have seen her circumstances and gotten her out of a bad situation. Who knows what might have happened if someone had stepped in. What pain and loss she might have avoided. "You know I'm a nurse, so who better to take care of you?"

"I told you. I take care of myself."

Page well remembered what that was like. Making her own meals. Buying her own clothes with what little money she had. Taking care of her own needs because her parents had checked out of her life early on. She took a seat in the chair beside Ruby's hospital bed. "How long have you been doing that?"

Ruby looked down at her hands. "Almost a year. My mom died, and they put me in this horrible foster home back in Oklahoma. I ran away as soon as I could." She sat up straighter in the bed. "You're not going to send me back there, are you?"

"No." She hoped she wouldn't have to.

She wilted back into the pillows. "I won't go. I'll run away before that happens."

"What happened after you left the home?"

"I started to make my way here. My mom told me stories about when she met my dad here. It wasn't like I had anything keeping me in Oklahoma." She sniffed and seemed to be holding back tears. "My boyfriend took off when I told him about the baby."

"Have you decided what you want to do about the baby?"

"I don't know. I keep changing my mind."

"That's okay."

Ruby looked her over. "What happens if I agree to live with you?"

"You take care of the baby you're carrying, and I'll watch over you. At least for now."

Ruby shrugged. "Maybe that could work."

Page patted her bald head. "You should know that I'm fighting cancer."

Ruby glanced up at her head. "Figured that was what it is. So do you get sick a lot?"

"Sometimes. But I'm still able to take care of us. They wouldn't let me keep working here if I couldn't." She moved and sat on the edge of her seat. "So what do you think?"

Ruby nodded. "I guess."

It wasn't a lot, but it was better than a refusal.

WITH THE FILE saved on his office computer, Mateo turned off the machine and prepared to leave. He wasn't due in court until Wednesday, so he still had plenty of time to prepare his opening argument. His client, a twelve-year-old accused of tagging graffiti on a freeway bridge, was at least willing to work with him on his defense. The memory of Scotty made him stop and reflect, but he shook it off as he picked up his briefcase.

Outside, he pressed the button on the key fob to unlock his car door just as his phone chirped. He brought the phone up to his ear without glancing at the screen. "Mateo Lopez."

"Do you always answer your phone so professionally?" his sister, Lulu, asked with a giggle. "Or are you always working?"

"More like the second one. What's up?"

A pause. "I've got some news, and I don't know how you're going to take it."

A bunch of alternatives bounced through his brain. "Your husband got a promotion, and you're moving out of state?"

"Don't even joke about that." His sister sighed. "Dad's dating somebody."

Mateo missed the step down from the curb and almost fell onto his car. “Dad is what?”

“Dating. Some lady from church. Tia Laurie called and asked me if I knew, but I swear I didn’t. He hasn’t said a word to me. You?”

He’d had dinner with his dad last night, but he hadn’t mentioned anything like dating someone. Hadn’t said anything about forgetting his wife and Mateo’s mother. “No. Is Tia Laurie sure about this? That doesn’t sound like something Dad would do. He still loves Mom.”

“He can love Mom and still date other women. She’s been dead for thirteen years, Mateo. He’s probably lonely.”

Lulu made it sound like it was a foregone conclusion that their father would make such a ludicrous decision. “Or she’s a gold digger.”

“Then she’s looking in the wrong place, isn’t she?” Lulu took a deep breath and then let it out. “Can you call and ask him?”

Why did he have to be the one to call him? Lulu was just as capable of talking to their father, even if Mateo had a closer relationship with him. “Why don’t you do it?”

“Because you’re his son, and he tells you things that he doesn’t share with me.”

“You’re his princess and have him wrapped around your finger.”

“Please, Mateo. I think we need to know, don’t you?”

No, he didn’t need to know. Frankly, Mateo would rather stay blissfully ignorant. His phone beeped from another incoming call. “I gotta go. It’s a client.”

“Call him.”

“Maybe.” He’d mull this over for a few days, or a week, before talking to their father. “Love you.” He hung up with his sister. “Mateo Lopez.”

“Good, you answered. I need some advice.”

He frowned, trying to place the familiar voice. “I’m sorry. Who is this?”

“Oh, it’s Page. I need a lawyer. Stat.”

He smirked at the thought of her contacting him when it wasn’t too long ago that she wouldn’t give him the time of day. Or the time to apologize properly. “Are you in jail? Do you need to be bailed out?”

"It's not for me. Uh, it is a little. I need a family lawyer."

He opened his car and got inside. "Page, what have you gotten yourself into?"

"That's the thing. I'm not sure what I'm about to do. All I know is that this girl needs somebody, and I want that somebody to be me."

"You're talking in code and I'm not following. What do you need me for exactly?"

It was several seconds before she finally answered. "I have a patient who's a minor that I'd like released into my care, but I don't have the first clue about how to go about it."

Did this woman know what she was asking? Did she realize what she was about to take on? "Released into your care?"

"Yes, I want to be her foster mother. Can you help me?"

"I can. But let me ask you a question—why did you call me?"

A pause on the other end, then her voice was soft, hesitant. "Because Sherri says you're the best lawyer, and that's what I need. The best."

"And the personal stuff?"

"We can keep this professional, can't we?"

He could. But even as they made plans to meet, he couldn't help but wonder why she'd even considered him in the first place.

CHAPTER THREE

PAGE PACED HER living room, pausing every few minutes to glance out the front window for Mateo's car. She checked her watch. He said he'd been close to her neighborhood. Was she crazy to think she could do this? To foster a pregnant teenager while she struggled with her own health issues? Would a judge even sign off on this?

A car pulled to the curb, and she sprinted to the front door and pulled it open.

Mateo strode up the walk and the two steps to her home. He gave her a nod and entered the house. "Thanks for agreeing to meet with me."

His scent of spice tickled her nose. She took a deep breath and let it out. She had to get her awareness of him under control.

"Page, do you realize what you're asking?"

She didn't need to think about her answer. "Yes."

He shook his head as if she was clueless. "You're talking about accepting responsibility for the welfare of an adolescent that you barely know."

"If you knew a child needed you, would you step in and do something or would you let her get lost in the system?" She stared at him hard. "Sherri's told me about all the work you've done with the youth in the community, so I know what you'd say. Now I'm in the position to help this girl, so please show me how."

He sighed and put his briefcase on the sofa next to him. "You'd be on the hook for her physical, financial and emotional well-being. Why would you put that on your shoulders when you have so much else to deal with?"

She couldn't help but start to take this personally. "Did you ask Dez the same questions when Marcus needed a foster home? I'm just as capable."

"I'm questioning you because a judge will be asking you these same things when we get to court."

"You said *when* we get to court, not *if*. Does that mean you'll help me?" She gave him a smile, relief settling her nervous belly.

"Yes, I'll take your case, but you shouldn't get too confident in our chances." He flipped open his briefcase, pulled out a thin stack of paper and handed it to her. It was an application for emergency foster-care placement. He nodded toward it. "Fill in as much as you can now, and I'll reach out to a contact I have in Child and Family Services. Brittney will make sure we get this fast-tracked. When will Ruby be released from the hospital?"

She wondered if the contact was a girlfriend, then dismissed the thought. "They're keeping her overnight, but because of her youth, maybe two days to be safe. We have about a day to make this happen." She got a pen from a mug that sat on her kitchen counter. Taking a seat on a stool, she started to complete the form. Name. Address. References. She brought up her head. "References?"

Mateo walked over to her. "People who will vouch for you. April, I'm assuming.

My cousin, Sherri. Do you have any family?"

Page thought of her parents. The last thing she needed was her mother trying to talk her out of this. And her father had no contact with her. "None that I want involved in this. You'd agree if you knew my mom. That won't hurt my chances, will it?"

"It would look better if she could be included, but it's not crucial."

She perused the rest of the application. "I fill this out, you call your friend, then what?"

"I can get a home study done pretty quickly. We'll get you fingerprinted and a criminal background check completed tonight, I hope. After that, it's in the social worker's hands." He brought out his phone and made a call. "Hey, Britt. Mind if I ask a favor?"

He walked out of earshot, so she returned to the application. It asked her about her financial details and medical history. She paused before writing *cancer* in the appropriate section. That wouldn't keep her from being able to care for Ruby, would it? It had already claimed so much from her, that she didn't need this to be stripped away, too.

MATEO ENDED HIS phone call and found Page working on the application. Her bald head bent over the form, she scribbled answers and didn't seem aware of him watching her. What was she thinking? She had bigger problems to worry about than some pregnant teenager. She needed to stay focused on fighting cancer, not look after some girl she didn't really know.

And yet, he admired her for it. How many able-bodied and healthy people turned and looked the other way rather than make a difference in a needy child's life?

She glanced up at him—big hazel-green eyes in a thin, pale face. She handed him the form. "Can you check it over to make sure I've filled in everything?"

He took the paper and examined it, reading it over with a critical eye. She'd given more than enough information, and he had a feeling that it would get approved despite her health issues if he got the case in front of the right judge. "You're sure you want to do this?"

Page nodded. “I haven’t changed my mind. I’m even more determined to help her.”

“You haven’t answered why.”

She took a deep breath and let it out slowly. “I was just like her at that age. Alone. Terrified. I ran away from home several times and lived on the streets until a cop found me and took me back. Maybe if an adult had seen my living situation, things might have turned out differently. I might not have married the first man who I thought could rescue me.”

He looked at her for a long moment, seeing the grief in her eyes. There was so much more to her than he’d realized before. She didn’t need to be rescued because she took matters into her own hands. Did she not see that? He glanced at his watch. “I have a few friends at the police department who can take your fingerprints and run the criminal background check now. Do you have any plans tonight?”

She gasped and stood up quickly. Too quickly. “I have to call April to let her know I won’t be making it to dinner. How long do you think this will take?”

"After we get you fingerprinted, you should ready a room for Ruby. The more prepared you are for her to enter your home, the better."

She nodded. "I'll fix up the guest room. Not that I have many guests, but you know."

"That would be a good idea. We want to show the social worker that you've considered everything, including opening your home, as well as your life, for this girl." He put away his cell phone. "I can help you out with that."

He put a hand at the small of her back to nudge her out of the house. The contact, as light as it was, sent a bolt of awareness through him. What was happening to him? First, he'd been questioning what he always wanted to do with his life professionally, and now this. This was Page. He had no interest in her romantically.

And yet, as he drove her to the police station, he couldn't stop thinking about her. About everything she'd said back at the house. Sympathy for her story had opened his eyes to seeing her differently. Maybe he could see her like she'd asked him to.

As they entered the precinct, he gave a

wave to Sergeant Shelby Novakowski, who met him at the front desk and looked Page up and down. "What brings you by, counselor? Another client?"

"Yes, but not in the way you're thinking. Page needs to get fingerprinted, but for a criminal background check for her foster-care application."

Shelby turned to Page. "Foster care, huh? That's a tough gig. Are you sure you can handle it?"

Page bristled and gave a short nod. "I'm tougher than I look."

"Good. You'll need to be." She winked at Mateo and motioned to an empty interrogation room. "Go ahead and take a seat. I'll see to this myself."

"Don't you have staff for this kind of thing?" Page asked.

Shelby laughed and pointed again to the room. "Consider this a favor. Now, go. Sit. I'll be right there."

As Page had her fingerprints taken and the data entered into the system, and filled out the necessary paperwork, he joked with one of the cops on duty. It felt good to be at the station for a different reason than bail-ing a client out. He was relaxed and could chat with the officers, most of whom he knew by name.

Once everything was taken care of at the station, Mateo escorted her back to his car. Page fastened her seat belt and turned to look at him. “Do you know all the cops?”

“I know quite a few, but then that’s part of my job.”

He drove them back to her house and volunteered to make up the guest bed with fresh linens. As he watched her prepare her place for her new charge, he had to admit Page was an interesting mix of strength and vulnerability, and he was drawn to her.

So, there he was, tucking the ends of a cotton blanket underneath a mattress because he couldn’t leave her to do it alone.

Page put her hands on her hips and surveyed the room. “This will do for now. Ruby and I can always go shopping if we want to later.”

“You realize that you have a lot of big hoops to jump through first, right? This isn’t a guaranteed placement. There’s a chance that she’ll have to stay in another home before she can come here while we get everything approved."

Page paused in smoothing the surface of the blanket and looked up at him. "I thought you said we could get this fast-tracked so she could come here."

"That doesn't mean it's overnight."

Her optimism seemed to fade a little, and she sagged onto the edge of the bed. "Oh. I guess I figured you could make it happen that way."

"I'm a criminal lawyer, not a miracle worker." She looked up at him with those big eyes, and he felt a punch in his belly. He knew he'd do everything he could to make this happen for her. He sighed. "I'll do the best I can."

"Ruby is alone and pregnant, and I feel for her. No one should ever be alone in the world. I want to be sure she's safe."

Mateo knew the feeling. Despite his own reservations regarding her health and her ability to care for herself, much less someone else, he wanted to help Page in this quest to provide a home for a homeless teenager.

PAGE HAD THE following day off, but she arrived at the hospital early and waved at her coworkers before walking down the hall to Ruby's room. She found the teen dozing with the television on, so Page picked up the remote control from the bedside table and turned the TV off. Ruby opened one eye to glare at her. "Hey, I was watching that."

She highly doubted that. "How are you feeling today?"

Ruby rubbed her rounded belly and shrugged. "Okay, I guess. The pains haven't started again, so that's a good thing, right?"

"Very good." Page looked up and peered into Ruby's eyes. "Your color looks better. Have you seen the doctor this morning?"

"She stopped by an hour or so ago." Ruby shifted in the hospital bed and reached behind her for a pillow. Page stepped forward and helped her get more comfortable. "She thinks I can get out of here later today or tomorrow morning, but they're waiting on some test."

"Sounds about right." She sat in the chair next to the bed. "I've been working all night to get a place ready for you at my house. Do you still want to do that?"

Ruby looked at her. "I guess."

Page doubted she could have gotten anything more enthusiastic from her. Ruby appeared to be jaded and cynical no matter what, albeit for good reason. "We're just waiting on social services to sign off on my application, but my friend Mateo, he's a lawyer, is hoping to get that finalized by tomorrow."

Ruby's brow furrowed. "What happens if it isn't, and they kick me out of here?"

"You could end up in another foster home."

Ruby started to shift as if she was going to get out of the bed. "Oh, no. I'm not doing that again."

Page put a hand on her shoulder, wanting to reassure the girl, but she realized it was a feeble attempt. If Ruby wanted to leave, she could. "It would only be a night or two until you can stay with me."

Ruby grasped Page's hand. "Don't make me go to a foster home, please."

The fear in the girl's eyes made Page even

more determined to bring this girl home with her. "I'm doing my best."

Ruby nodded.

Page took a seat on the hospital bed. "Can you tell me anything more about your family?"

She kept her gaze on the window across the room. "What family?"

Page was losing patience with the girl. How would she ever help someone who didn't meet her halfway? "They're going to check out your story, so be sure you're telling us everything. No grandparents? Aunts or uncles?"

Ruby folded her hands in her lap and kept her gaze on them. "It was just my mom and me until she died. If there were any relatives, she didn't tell me one word about them."

"How did she die?"

Ruby raised her eyes to Page. "Don't matter now. She's just dead."

"Did she know about your baby?"

"I found out just before she died. I didn't know how to tell her. I didn't want her to be disappointed in me."

"I'm sure she would have loved you anyway." When Ruby nodded, Page could tell that the bond between the two had been strong. "I don't want you to think that I'd be taking your mom's place if you come and stay with me. Maybe you could think of me as a friend, though." She pulled a notebook and pen from her purse. "And I thought you could write a letter for the judge telling him where you want to live."

Ruby took the notebook and opened to a clean page. "You mean with you."

"I thought it would help our case."

Ruby peered at her. "You really want this?"

"I do."

"What about when the baby comes?"

Page already knew the answer. "We'll figure it out together, no matter your decision."

Ruby gave a short nod then started to write.

A nurse entered the room to check Ruby's vitals, ending the conversation. Page stepped back so that Tiffany could check over Ruby. She gave her a nod before leaving the room. Ruby raised an eyebrow at the exchange. "Friend of yours?"

Hardly. "I think she's after my job."

"There's always someone who wants what you got." Ruby nodded as if she was the older and wiser one.

"You've got that right."

MATEO HUNG UP from his phone call with Brittney and pumped his fist in the air. Together, they had been able to work a miracle. He scrolled through his contacts and found Page's name. He pressed his finger on it and waited for the call to connect. "It's Mateo. Where are you?"

"With Ruby at the hospital."

"Do you think you can meet me at your house ASAP? Judge Bond has agreed to hear our case at three this afternoon, but the social worker wants to complete a home inspection before that." He glanced at his watch. "She can meet us at your house within the hour. Does that work?"

"Yes, of course." She muffled the phone and relayed the news to the girl. "Thank you, Mateo. Ruby thanks you, too."

"Let's take this one step at a time before you get too excited. We still have a ways to go."

Mateo just hoped that the judge would agree that Page was Ruby's best option.

HE ARRIVED AT Page's house and saw Brittney's car parked in the driveway. He walked up to the front door, found it open and stepped inside. "Hello?"

Page popped her head from around the corner and waved him down the hallway to the guest room. He entered and greeted Brittney. "Thanks for being on the ball with this, Britt."

"Don't thank me yet. We still have to convince the judge." She turned and gave a bright smile to Page. "But I think we'll get what we want."

Page sighed and placed a hand to her chest. "I want to do everything I can for Ruby."

Brittney left to inspect the rest of the house. Mateo stepped closer to Page. "Has she opened up more about her family?"

"According to her, there isn't any. None she knows of anyway. It was always her and her mom until the mom died. She did say she knows her father's name. Thomas Burns." She rubbed her bare arms and looked down at her T-shirt and shorts. "Guess I should get changed for court."

"The judge is going to be more interested in what you have in your heart than what clothes you have on your body." He scanned her from head to toe. "On the other hand, it wouldn't hurt to put on something a little more dressy."

She nodded and went to change. Mateo walked back to the living room, where he found Brittney making notes on her tablet. She clutched the tablet to her chest. "No peeking. You know the rules."

He knew very well what they were up against, but that didn't mean he wouldn't try to get an advantage. "Do you think she's got a chance?"

"More than a chance if I have anything to say about it. Have you seen how clean and organized this place is? I'm tempted to hire her to come and take a stab at my apartment." Brittney walked into the kitchen and opened a cupboard. "The spices are organized alphabetically. And the cans by food group. Don't even get me started on the color-coded closets and linens."

"It takes more than organization to convince a judge."

"She's got stellar references from her friends to provide emotional support, although I wish she had stronger family ties." She typed in more notes. "But then maybe she can identify with coming from a broken family like Ruby does."

"And the cancer?"

Brittney stopped typing and looked at him. "That's the wild card in this. She's in midtreatment, but I have a letter from her doctor that states she is physically able to care for a child. So that's got to stand for something."

Impressed that Page had thought to get the letter before he had, he gave a nod. "Let's hope the judge sees it the same way."

Mateo stared as Page entered the living room. She had put on a simple black sleeveless dress and tied a silk floral scarf around her head. She frowned and looked down at her outfit. "What's wrong? Is the scarf too much? I don't usually wear one, but I thought it might not hurt."

Brittney made an amused noise next to him and moved on to check the basement.

He took a few steps closer to Page. "Nothing. You're fine."

She kept the frown on her face and put a hand on her hip. "The look on your face said otherwise."

He took a deep breath and reminded himself she was a client. He shouldn't be thinking that the dark color of her dress made her eyes look like emeralds. Or that the scarf made those eyes look huge. He cleared his throat and adjusted his tie. Was it hot in here?

"Did Brittney say anything about my case?"

"We both agree that it looks promising. Do you have a statement prepared?"

She shook her head. "Sort of, but I figured I'd speak from the heart when the time comes. Do you think I should write something?"

"That's usually best." His phone chimed, and he took it out of his pocket to check the display. Lulu was texting to remind him about calling his dad. It would have to wait. "We won't be in a courtroom but rather the judge's chambers. It will be less intimidating, hopefully."

"She's dead set against going into a foster home."

"We'll do our best."

Brittney returned to the living room and approached them. "I've finished my report, so I'll see you later at the courthouse." She put her tablet in her purse then put a hand on Page's arm. "Good luck. This girl will be lucky to have you."

Page thanked her and Brittney departed. He noticed Page sat down quickly on the sofa and doubled over. "I don't think I've ever been this nervous. Not even when I got married."

Mateo sat next to her and put an arm around her shoulders. "It'll be okay. I'll be with you through this. You won't do it on your own."

She nodded against his shoulder. "Thank you."

He dropped his arm, and they sat in an uncomfortable silence. They had a few hours before they had to appear in the judge's chambers. "Page, about what you said last week. About how I don't see you."

She reached up and removed the scarf from her head. "Yes?"

"You were right." He looked deep into her eyes. "I haven't seen you as a person. Not really. And I'm sorry for that."

She swallowed. "Thank you."

"But all of this the last couple of days has opened my eyes."

"And?"

He wasn't sure what to say at first. She looked so hopeful, but he couldn't give her false expectations. "I'd like for us to be friends."

The light dimmed in her eyes. "Friends. Sure." The smile on her face looked forced. "Who couldn't use more friends?"

MATEO DROVE THEM both to the courthouse since Page hadn't been able to concentrate on anything beyond what the judge's decision might be. She had to convince the judge that she could take care of Ruby. Had to show him that it was in the girl's best interest for her to stay with Page. She tried to think of what she would say when the time came, but words didn't seem to stick in her brain. All that filled it was the image of Ruby alone in that hospital bed.

They pulled into a garage and Mateo

parked. He turned off the engine and glanced over at her. He'd been so helpful through this process. Had it really been twenty-four hours since she'd met Ruby and set all of this in motion? She'd never been impulsive, but this certainly qualified. Mateo put a hand over hers and squeezed. "No matter what, it's going to be okay."

The feel of his strong hand on hers made the butterflies in her belly slow their flight. "What if the judge doesn't see it my way?"

"Then we go to plan B."

She raised an eyebrow at this. "Do we have a plan B?"

Mateo grinned. "We'll think of something."

He got out of the car, and Page opened the passenger-side door. And then he was there with a hand to help her out. She took it and didn't let go as they walked out of the garage and crossed the street toward the courthouse.

Once inside, they waited a few moments until the steel elevator doors opened. They entered, along with several other people, and Mateo pressed the button. Crowded in, Page found herself squished to his side. She kept her gaze forward, but was aware of how his breath caught as the elevator started its ascent. She could smell the aftershave he wore, a spicy citrus scent. His presence alone lent her courage and strength.

He was right. If this didn't work, they would figure out a plan B. Ruby didn't have anyone else to be her advocate. To make the decisions that would help her and her unborn baby. Page wanted desperately to be able to help her.

She'd wrestled with the question of why the previous night. As the first rays of dawn appeared, she realized that she'd hoped for someone to step into her life as a teenager and care for her. That she'd dreamed of an adult who would see the neglect in her situation at home and stand up for her, and provide a home where she didn't have to worry about the next meal, or having clean clothes to wear to school. It hadn't happened for her, but she could do that for Ruby. She couldn't lose this chance.

The elevator doors opened, and Mateo ushered her forward. They walked down a long hallway to an unmarked door. Mateo rapped on it and took a step back. An older man with graying hair and a beard answered. He extended a hand to Mateo, who shook it. "Mr. Lopez, on time as always."

The man turned to her. "Ms. Kosinski. I'm Judge Frederick Bond, welcome."

She put her hand in his.

With a broad sweep of his arm, he stepped back and allowed them to enter his chambers. They found Brittney sitting in a chair in front of a massive desk. The judge moved behind it and indicated the other empty chair. Page took a seat while Mateo stood behind her. Judge Bond opened a manila folder and perused the paperwork. He glanced up to peer at her. She folded her hands in her lap and prayed that she looked trustworthy. After reading through the file, he closed it and spoke to Brittney. "Has the state reached a recommendation on Ms. Kosinski's application for emergency foster-care placement?"

"The state has, Your Honor." Brittney perched on the edge of her chair. "We believe that she is an excellent candidate to receive the minor, Ruby Wilson, into her care. As you can see from her application, she is employed as a nurse at Detroit General and can provide for the physical and emotional needs of the child. She has prepared her home for this placement. We believe she also has a strong support network of friends who will help her if she needs it." Brittney pointed to the file. "Ruby has written her own statement as well, indicating her desire to live with Ms. Kosinski."

The judge perused more of the file. "I understand the minor is pregnant and two months from delivery. Are you prepared to take on the responsibility of an infant as well?"

Page nodded. "Yes, Your Honor. Although she hasn't decided what she plans to do once the baby arrives."

The judge looked at Page. "And how are you feeling?"

Mateo cleared his throat. "Dr. Frazier is prepared to testify that Ms. Kosinski is in good physical condition to care for a minor."

The judge put a finger on his upper lip and rubbed it. "I was asking your client."

They all turned to face her. She gave a

nod. “Today is a good day for me, Your Honor.”

“And how much longer will you be receiving chemotherapy treatments?”

“Hopefully another month or two, and then the doctor will assess how well I’m doing.” She took a deep breath. “I understand you may have reservations regarding my cancer, but please let me state that it won’t interfere with being able to take care of Ruby or her baby.”

“Good. And why are you applying to be her foster mother?”

“In my application—”

Judge Bond held up his hand. “I read what you wrote there, but I want to hear it from your own mouth. Why are you pursuing this, Ms. Kosinski? Is it the monthly stipend you’d receive from the state? Or are you one of those do-gooders with their hearts on their sleeves trying to save the world?”

“I’m only trying to save one girl. Ruby.” Page took a deep breath, trying to sort out what she should say to convince him. She decided on the truth and pulled out the sheet of paper where she’d written her thoughts earlier. "Given different circumstances, I might have been her when I was her age. I know what it's like to have no one and to wish that someone would see me. I've gone hungry and lived on the streets a time or two. I don't want that life for her. I want her to feel loved and cared for. Her and her baby."

Mateo put a hand on her shoulder and gripped it lightly. "Your Honor, Ms. Kosinski has a job that provides more than she needs. The stipend has no consideration on her decision to be a foster parent for Ruby."

"And there is no family member who can step forward and take care of the girl?"

Page shook her head. "None she knows of. She's quite alone."

Judge Bond gave a short nod. "I've decided to grant you temporary custody of Ruby Wilson." When Page smiled and clapped her hands together, he held up a finger. "Temporary only at this point, Ms. Kosinski. As it is, this is an emergency situation and the girl needs a home. In the meantime, I want a full investigation into her background to determine if there is no family member responsible for her. Until that time, Ms. Kosinski, you are granted full guardianship over her. If no relative is found, then we can discuss permanent placement."

"Thank you, Your Honor."

"Good luck, Ms. Kosinski. I have a feeling you're going to need it."

Page tamped down her excitement until they left the judge's chambers, then she threw her arms around Mateo and hugged him. "Thank you."

He tightened his arms around her. "I'm glad this went our way."

She missed the closeness when he let go of her, but she turned to Brittney. "Thank you as well. I can't tell you how grateful I am that you jumped on this so fast."

"I'll be reaching out to you once Ruby is released from the hospital. We'll set up a time to interview her about her family. Also, I'll be checking in randomly to be sure the placement is going well."

Brittney nodded to Mateo and was soon out of sight.

Page couldn't hold back her next question any longer. "Do you think we could go and tell Ruby now?"

Mateo's smile was warm and wide. She was sure it mirrored her own. He drove them to the hospital and accompanied her to Ruby's room. But when she pushed open the door, the room was empty. Page frowned and went to the nurse's station. "Tiffany, where's Ruby?"

The nurse shrugged. "She was released and left. The doctor didn't see a reason to keep her any longer."

Page turned to Mateo. "Where could she have gone?"

CHAPTER FOUR

PAGE TRIED TO figure out where a girl with nowhere to go would flee. She sighed. "She couldn't have gone far." She sprinted for the hospital exit, Mateo on her heels.

"Page, let's take a moment and think about this."

She kept her pace quick. "No. The longer we wait, the farther she gets." She was almost to the sliding glass doors. "I have to find her."

"Maybe she doesn't want to be found."

"We all want to be found." Page knew something about trying to hide but wishing someone would truly see her, to save her. Not that she had any illusions about saving Ruby. She only wanted to give the girl a chance.

Outside, she stopped and put her hands on her hips, surveying the area around them. Parking lot, cars, grassy quad and concrete sidewalks. Everything open. “If I wanted to get away and think, presumably, where would I go?”

“A park. A mall, maybe. Any place I wouldn’t stand out. I’d want to blend in, go unnoticed.”

Page turned to Mateo. “You’re full of surprises, Mateo.”

“Hey, I was an angry, troubled teenager once. Weren’t you?”

“I figured you would be the perfect kid, all A student and chores done on time. Don’t tell me I have to take you down from that pedestal.”

Mateo put a hand on her arm and stopped her. “Are you sure that you want to do this, Page? Why has she suddenly changed her mind about living with you? You could be asking for more trouble than it’s worth.”

She pushed away his hand. “She needs me. And maybe I need her a little, too.”

She walked through the parking lot and kept walking. Ruby had to be nearby, she kept reminding herself. Mateo followed, pointing out a sign for a community garden just a few blocks north. They found Ruby on a rickety chair behind a large shed, eyes closed, a protective hand on her rounded belly.

Page approached and touched Ruby's hand. The teenager's eyes flew open, and she sprang forward.

"I'm not going to hurt you, Ruby." Page edged a little closer. "Why didn't you wait for me? Did you think I'd forgotten about you? That I wasn't coming?" Page took a deep breath and released it, needing to reestablish trust between them. "When I make a promise, I keep it. You have to know that about me. The two of us aren't going to work very well together if we don't believe in each other."

Ruby was silent and wiped a tear from her cheek, but finally looked at Page. "I thought maybe the judge denied your application. I can't go to another home like before. I figured I'd run away again."

"You don't have to worry about that because the judge said you can stay with me until we find your family."

The tension in the girl's shoulders lessened noticeably. "I told you. I don't got any."

"Well, then I guess you're stuck with

me." Page offered the girl a smile that she returned. She held out a hand to the teenager. "Let's go home."

Ruby still didn't seem convinced. Her eyes darted between her and Mateo. "I don't know. What if I make a mess? Or what if you get mad at me and yell?"

"What if I snore? Or I cook something you don't like? We won't know unless we try." She held out her hand and almost did a victory dance when Ruby grasped it. "Remember my friend Mateo? He's going to drive us home."

Ruby wriggled her eyebrows. "Boyfriend?"

She snorted. "Just a friend." They all walked together to the parking lot.

Ruby whispered to her, "He's cute. You're sure he's just a friend?"

"Oh, yeah," she reassured Ruby, but she couldn't help but notice Mateo's grin.

MATEO FIGURED THAT Page and Ruby would need even more time to bond if that relationship was going to have a chance. Being a criminal lawyer, he'd seen enough situations, including adoptions and foster-parent placements, to know that the first twenty-four hours could be critical.

Ruby gave him the once-over then said to Page, “He doesn’t look old enough to be a lawyer.”

“Trust me. He’s a good one.” Page shaded her eyes with her hand and smiled at him.

Page had said the girl was seven months pregnant, but Ruby looked ready to deliver now. He hoped she could get settled at Page’s before that happened. He hit his fob to unlock the car doors, and Page and Ruby both got in the back seat.

“So I’m your chauffeur?” he mumbled and got into the driver’s seat. He started to drive them to Page’s house when someone’s stomach growled. He looked at them in the back seat via the rearview mirror. “Should we stop for dinner?”

Page glanced at Ruby, then at him. “Do you have time? Don’t you have another client to see?”

“You’re my only client today.” He checked his mirrors and changed lanes. “Do you like Mexican food? My uncle owns a great place not far from here.”

Ruby nodded. “My favorite. Unless you don’t like it, Page?”

“I love tacos, so that sounds great to me.”

Tío Javier met him at the door when they walked inside the cantina. They embraced before Javier spoke to Page and Ruby. “You brought dates?”

“Clients.” Mateo introduced them and then Javier ushered them to a table. Mateo took a menu, but his uncle grabbed it from him. “I’ll cook you something special.” He turned to the women. “Feeling adventurous?”

Page looked at Mateo, her eyes showing a little apprehension. He gave a small nod to her. “Easy on the spices, though. They’re not used to what we like.”

Javier nodded and headed straight for the kitchen while his Tía Sara brought a basket of freshly fried tortilla chips and a bowl of salsa. Ruby dug into the chips and salsa and groaned. “This is my *favorite* part of eating at a Mexican place.”

Page took a chip and broke it in half before dipping it into the salsa, only letting a little of the sauce get onto the chip. She put it into her mouth and chewed. Her eyes closed and she smiled.

"You like it?" he asked.

She nodded and dipped her other half in the salsa, putting a little more onto this one. "I have to be careful with onions and spices, but this is fabulous."

Ruby asked, "Why do you have to be careful?"

Mateo and Page exchanged glances before she took a deep breath. "I just have to be careful with what I eat. Sensitive stomach."

"Because of the cancer, right?"

Page gave a quick nod. "Certain spices make me more nauseous than others. But this seems to be okay."

"Ugh, I don't know what I'd do if I couldn't eat what I want." Ruby took a chip and added some hot sauce along with the salsa.

"Speaking of food, we should go grocery shopping. What do you like?"

But the conversation got cut short when Javier brought platters of food. They filled their bellies, enjoying every amazing taste.

In between mouthfuls, they covered a

wide range of topics. At one point, Page narrowed her eyes at Ruby. "You like musicals?"

The teen stopped the fork halfway to her mouth. "Why is that so shocking? My mom played them on the stereo while we cleaned the apartment every Saturday morning. *South Pacific. The Sound of Music.* Even *The Phantom of the Opera* and *Les Mis.*" She put the food in her mouth and continued talking. "And on Sundays she put on gospel music. It was our thing, I guess."

"What can you tell me about your mom?" Mateo asked. "Did you have any aunts or uncles? Grandparents?"

Mateo knew that it was too soon for the question the way Ruby's face suddenly seemed to shutter. He regretted putting the questions out there. He reached under the table and took Page's hand in his, squeezing it as if to tell her he was sorry for asking.

Page gripped his hand and waved her other in front of her face. "We can talk about that later. Let's get to know more about you. What about books? Do you like to read?"

And the teenager started talking about

the last novel she'd been able to get her hands on before coming to Michigan.

WHILE MATEO PAID their bill and Ruby visited the restroom for the fifth time, Page checked her cell phone. She found a text from April. How'd it go?

She's coming home with me. But I don't know anything about taking care of a teenage girl.

Page paused and erased the second part of the text. She wasn't ready to admit that she was feeling in over her head, although the idea of being responsible for Ruby had started to sink in. It was August, and schools were out. But she'd have to get her registered for the fall semester. And what school would she go to? What grade was she even in?

Ruby had nothing with her when she'd been admitted into the ER, so she was going to need clothes, shoes, personal items. Page didn't like shopping much, and that idea alone made her take a step back. What had she been thinking?

When Ruby emerged from the restroom, a hand holding her belly, all thoughts fled Page's mind except one: take care of her and the baby. Page approached her and put a hand on the girl's shoulder. "You feeling okay?"

Ruby looked up at her and nodded. "I think I ate too much. But it was so good, I couldn't help it."

Mateo's uncle's face split into a smile. "I like this one. You bring them both back to me and I fatten them up good."

Mateo tucked his wallet into his pocket. "Well, Ruby, you've won my uncle over. How about we go buy you some clothes and things? Then I'll take you to Page's house so you both can rest."

Page frowned. "Seriously, don't you have clients other than us?" She didn't want to monopolize his time if he was needed elsewhere.

"I told you. You're my only client today." He walked to the front door of the restaurant and held it open for them both.

Page paused as she passed by him. "I can take her on my own."

"You look like you could fall asleep on

your feet. I'd just take you back to the house and suggest you shop later, but Ruby definitely needs a few things right now." He glanced at the girl, who was waiting by his car. "I've got the impression she's been wearing that same top and pants for days, if not weeks."

"Fine. You can still play chauffeur, but add it to my bill."

He saluted her, walked to his car and helped Ruby inside. Page knew he was only doing his job, but sometime during their day together it had begun to feel personal. He'd finally admitted that he wanted to be friends, but she sensed there could be more. Besides, they had a pregnant teenager chaperoning them, so it could hardly be construed as anything romantic. Yet the way he'd held her hand under the table…

She got in the car beside Ruby in the back seat.

When Mateo pulled up in front of a store that carried everything from clothing to groceries, she let out a sigh, thankful it wasn't a mall, and they could get everything they needed in one stop. Mateo left them to their task and opted to go on a solo mission.

Unfortunately, the store didn't carry maternity clothing. Still, Ruby was able to get some oversize T-shirts and roomy pants, as well as a couple of bras and underwear that would get her through a few days at least, until they could get to a department store with a maternity section. She also picked up some toiletries and magazines and a pair of sandals she could slide into. They hit the grocery section next and took their purchases to the registers near the front of the store. Page looked inside the cart. "Anything else you need that you can think of?"

Ruby gave a shrug. "Maybe."

"What is it?"

The girl let out a breath and pushed her hair out of her eyes. "That doctor friend of yours mentioned something about the baby needing vitamins or something."

"Prenatal vitamins? We can get some generic ones here until I can get you to a doctor who can prescribe you something better."

"Another doctor?" Ruby seemed shaken, but followed Page as she headed for the pharmacy. "I told you. I'm feeling fine. I don't need a doctor anymore."

"You need one now more than ever with a baby on the way."

"I got you, don't I? You're a nurse, so why do I need a doctor, too?"

Page found a bottle of prenatal vitamins and put them in the cart. "Sorry, kiddo. But you're not going to win this one. You'll see my friend Dr. Achatz. She's already familiar with your case, and she's one of the best."

Ruby groaned as Page added another bottle of folic acid. "I don't like taking a lot of stuff."

"This will be good for the baby. Trust me."

"I don't have a choice, do I?"

They returned to the registers, where Page noticed Mateo waiting for them with a bag. She quickly paid for everything in the cart and she and Ruby joined him. He handed the bag to Ruby. "I thought you might like this."

Ruby smiled and opened the bag. She took out a CD of a musical that Page had seen in New York City with her friends this past spring. The girl squealed and gave Mateo a hug. “Thanks.”

Mateo blushed and seemed uncomfortable with the attention. “You said you like musicals.”

“I’ve been dying to listen to this one.” She began humming one of the tunes and walked out of the store.

Page followed and said to Mateo, “You didn’t have to do that. Feeding us and buying gifts isn’t part of your legal services.”

“I know. But maybe I wanted to do something more.”

He drove them home and helped them get everything inside. Page walked him to the door, and he stood on the front porch, his hands in his pockets. “You’ll be okay?” he asked.

“I figure I’ll give Ruby the five-cent tour. Then we’ll both take a nap. We can hammer out rules and such later.” She took a step outside so that she was standing close to him. “Thank you for everything, Mateo.” Before she could stop herself, she kissed his cheek.

Mateo gulped visibly as she backed away. He stared into her eyes for a moment and took a step toward her. She wondered if he was about to kiss her.

But then he turned, walked away, got in his car and left, and she could only ask herself what had just happened?

MATEO PULLED INTO the driveway of the house he'd grown up in and parked behind his dad's car. He hadn't called ahead to see if his dad was home, but he wouldn't have known what to say if he had. When he'd left Page's place, he had been confused. Scared. And completely out of his league.

For a moment there, he'd been tempted to kiss her back. But not on her cheek. Thinking of her lips, he groaned and rubbed a hand over his eyes. He hadn't had friendship on his mind when she'd kissed him. He needed to stop thinking. That's what he needed to do.

He got out of the car and started walking up the driveway. By the time he made it to the front door, his dad was there waiting for him. He pulled Mateo inside the house and gave him a tight hug. "It's not Sunday. Did we have plans?"

Mateo patted the old man on the back. “Can’t I stop by and see how you’re doing?”

They broke apart and his dad narrowed his eyes. “One of your aunties talked about seeing me on a date with a woman, I bet.”

“Are you surprised? Lulu asked me to talk to you about it.” Mateo claimed a seat on the sofa and his dad took his usual seat in the recliner. “You haven’t dated anyone since Mom, so this is big news.”

His dad rubbed a hand along his jaw. “Not that big.”

Mateo would rather lose a dozen cases than talk about his dad’s love life, but here he was sitting in his childhood home talking about his dad dating. He blamed his sister. Lulu balked at the hard conversations, but he’d been having them with his dad for years. It was what had gotten him through his teenage years. He knew he could tell his dad anything and hoped it was a two-way street. “Is it serious, Dad?”

“It’s only been two dates.”

“You proposed to Mom on your first date.”

His dad sighed and sat on the edge of the seat, his hands on his knees. “A man gets lonely and thinks about how it might be nice to spend time with a smart woman who looks and smells good. That having someone to talk to over dinner sounds better than staring at an empty chair across the table and eating another frozen meal."

"That's all this is? Loneliness?"

"No. I'm saying it wrong." He looked out to the front lawn. "You kids are grown up. Lulu's married and ready to start her own family and you're busy with your job. I started to think about having something just for me." He paused and turned his head to face Mateo. "I'm not looking to replace your mom. Still, she also wouldn't want me to be sad and alone."

Mateo nodded. When his mom died, he hadn't expected his dad to die along with her. He'd still had to raise two kids and get them through college. He'd been there for everything for both him and his sister. Graduations, first dates, heartbreaks, Lulu's wedding. He would be around for much more.

"Will there be a third date?"

His dad grinned. "Maybe. She's a nice woman."

"Would the aunties approve?"

"The better question is whether they would approve of your dinner date today."

Tío Javier must have called. Mateo narrowed his eyes at this. "She's a client, nothing more."

His dad sniffed and gave a shrug. "Aren't you lonely, too? Don't you want to have dinner with a smart, pretty woman some time?"

"I'm not looking to date, Dad." He returned his father's grin. "I'll leave that to you."

His father colored, but shared the smile. "It's nice to have someone to spend time with. To take to dinner and a movie. You can't spend your whole life in the courtroom and your law books. I mean, the family's been worried about you. You seem to have closed yourself off to all that."

He opened his mouth to refute that view, but his dad had a point. He hadn't dated anyone seriously since Camilla, and that had been over five years ago. Not since law school. It wasn't that he wanted to be alone. He thought that it would be nice to be married and have a family someday.

Someday.

"Like I said, I'm not looking for anything more from Page than helping her with her case. And being her friend."

"And I've discovered that sometimes you find what you didn't even realize you'd been looking for in the first place."

RUBY PERCHED ON the edge of the bed and looked up at Page, who was hanging the clothing that they'd bought earlier. "I'm off work the day after tomorrow. We can go to the mall then and get you more clothes and things."

The girl wrinkled her nose. "The mall?"

Page turned to look at Ruby. "What's wrong with the mall? They'll have what we need."

"I hate shopping." The girl groaned and flopped back on the bed.

Page couldn't hide her smile at such a dramatic display. She closed the closet doors and took a seat on the bed next to Ruby. "I'll let you in on a secret. I do, too. I'd much rather pick something online and have it delivered. One click, and I'm done."

Ruby propped herself up. “Couldn’t we do that instead?”

“Absolutely.”

Page went and retrieved her laptop. Huddled together on the bed, they looked at several websites until Ruby found several items she liked. When Page got her credit card to make the purchase, Ruby started to rub her belly, something that Page noticed she did when she appeared to be thinking and was unsure of what to say. “What is it? Was there something else you’d like to order?”

Ruby shook her head and picked up a magazine from the plastic bag lying on the bed. “I’m good.”

“You can tell me anything.” Page motioned to the screen. “Did you change your mind about these?”

Ruby quit paging through the magazine and asked, “Why are you buying me a bunch of clothes if I won’t be here long?”

That’s what she was worried about? “You’ll be here for a while, at least. You said you didn’t have any family, but we need to confirm that. The search may not be easy or done quickly.”

"And what if we find him, and he doesn't want me?"

"You mean your dad?" Page peered into the girl's eyes. "What do you know about him?"

"I told you all I have is his name and Detroit. Mom didn't talk about him much." Ruby gave a shrug as if she didn't care, but the tight cords in her neck told Page otherwise. She scooted closer to the girl. "And what if we can't find him? Would I stay with you?"

"I promised to take care of you, and I'm not going to turn my back on that." She reached up and brushed the hair from Ruby's eyes. "I told you. You're stuck with me, kid."

Ruby still seemed skeptical, but gave a nod. "All right then. I'll find a way to pay you back for all this." She gestured to the online order on the laptop.

"You don't have to pay me back. This is part of my taking care of you."

"But this is too much." Ruby put her hand on Page's before she could finalize the order. "I shouldn't take all of this. Let's delete some items from the cart."

"No, I think we should get this. Besides, we don't know how anything will fit. What if we end up having to send some back?"

Ruby started to rub her belly again and Page put a hand over hers. "It's okay, Ruby. I want to do this for you."

The girl squeezed her hand. "Okay."

Page entered her credit-card information and completed the order. "Now, about this room. How would you like to decorate it?"

Ruby shook her head. "Not right now." She stretched out on the bed. "I think I have to take a nap."

Page shut the laptop and set it on the dresser. She removed a blanket from the closet and laid it over Ruby. "Sleep as long as you want. We can figure the rest out later."

The girl didn't say anything, but closed her eyes. Page watched her for a moment then left the room with her laptop. She kept the door ajar, just in case Ruby needed her.

She knew Ruby wasn't an infant who needed constant monitoring, but Page wasn't sure how else to do this. She didn't have a clue as to how to be a parent. It wasn't like she'd had great examples herself. She was floundering here.

She retreated to her room and lied down on her own bed. A nap sounded tempting, and she'd need to take better care of herself if she was going to be responsible for Ruby. She closed her eyes and tried to ignore the panic that came from that thought.

CHAPTER FIVE

The calendar indicated that Mateo had a free afternoon. Maybe he should go home to his condo and take a dip in the pool? When was the last time he'd had a moment to do something for himself? Instead, his cell phone vibrated and he answered the call. "Mateo Lopez." The caller didn't say anything at first. "Hello? You've reached Mateo Lopez. Is someone there?"

He took the phone from his ear and was about to press the button to hang up when the caller said, "I need a lawyer."

He took a seat behind his desk, grabbing a legal pad and pen. So much for the free afternoon. "How can I help you?"

"My son. He's been arrested on drug charges."

He put the pen back on the desk. He'd never taken a case with drug-related charges, but he knew a colleague who would. "I can give you the name of a very good lawyer who is better able to defend your son." He started to dig through his address book for Dave's information.

"No, my friend recommended you. She said you helped get the case against her son dropped."

"Who recommended me?"

"Silvia Delgado."

Mateo closed his eyes and wrote the name on the legal pad. He remembered the case well. Paolo had been caught with stolen merchandise, but it had been planted by a so-called friend. After producing the evidence that this friend was the real culprit, the DA had exonerated Paolo. "Her son wasn't facing charges to do with drugs. I'm afraid that I don't have any expertise in that area."

"But Silvia said..." The woman started to cry on the other end. "Preston is only fourteen. I can't have his whole life end now."

Mateo couldn't watch another kid get lost in a life of crime or drugs or poverty. It was too much to ask. He rubbed the bridge of his nose. "Like I said, I can give you Dave's number. He's better equipped to help you."

"Please, Mr. Lopez."

He read off Dave's information and repeated the phone number in case she hadn't written it down the first time.

The woman sighed. "If you're sure..."

"I am. Good luck." And he hung up before he could change his mind. He placed the phone on his desk and stared at it. His fingers twitched, wanting to reach out and call her back and yet...

He needed to figure out what kind of lawyer he really wanted to be. He'd started out taking cases for his family members; things like wills, prenup agreements, even a divorce. Then he'd had his first juvenile law case. He closed his eyes and could see the kid's face even though four years had passed. He couldn't forget how he'd looked sitting in this office beside his parents as they told him the facts of the arrest. Caught for vandalism to a school, a second offense even though the first one had been thrown out when the store owner had dropped the charges if Jimmy paid for the damages. This time, the school principal wasn't so forgiving. He wanted the kid prosecuted to the full extent of the law. And because of the amount of damage he'd caused, it could be considered a felony. The kid was fourteen and facing jail.

Mateo steepled his fingers and tapped his mouth with them. Because Jimmy's parents were going through a messy divorce, Mateo had been able to convince a judge that the kid needed counseling, rather than to serve time. Jimmy had also worked after school cleaning the building to pay back the cost of repairing the damages. He had just graduated from that school and was about to attend Michigan State to pursue a dual degree in education and psychology.

The case's outcome had convinced Mateo that he could turn his passion for rehabilitating these kids into a lucrative law career. But after four seemingly long years, it now left a bad taste in his mouth. He'd grown weary of excuses and attitudes. His passion had become his curse.

Maybe what he needed was a new passion, a new focus. He could go back to criminal law, focusing as he had on taking cases like Page's, where he could help to forge families. Unfortunately, the juvenile crime statistics of his neighborhood held more lucrative opportunities.

With a sigh, he closed his laptop and placed it in his canvas messenger bag. He swung it over one shoulder, left his office and locked all three dead bolts, then left the building and walked out to the parking lot, where heat shimmered off the blacktop. He rolled down all the windows after he started the car, letting the faint breeze attempt to cool the interior.

He took a drive down Lakeshore Drive, watching the boats on Lake St. Clair. What if he got on a boat and just left? Start over somewhere else where he wouldn't have to face these kids who needed a champion? He could go where kids didn't have to live a life with so many challenges. He'd find happiness there, right?

He parked and left his car at Lake Front Park while he walked to the shore. He stood, hands in his pockets, staring at the eastern horizon while he contemplated what to do next. Because, to be honest, he didn't have a clue.

RUBY'S LEGS SWUNG back and forth as she sat on the examination table, waiting for Dr. Achatz to come into the room. Page reached out and touched Ruby's knee. "Nervous?"

"Kind of."

Page sat back in the plastic molded chair and returned to the magazine article she'd been pretending to read. She was unable to focus on the words because her mind raced with questions and worries. This guardian stuff wasn't for wimps. You had to be strong and pretend you knew what you were doing. Good thing Page had been doing that for years.

The door opened and Dr. Achatz entered with a smile. "Ruby, it's good to see you again."

The teen girl grunted a response while Page stood. "We appreciate you seeing us so quickly. I wanted to make sure both Ruby and the baby are doing okay."

"I heard you took temporary guardianship for her. Good for you." Dr. Achatz put her stethoscope in her ears and listened to Ruby's heartbeat. She nodded and felt Ruby's neck. "How are you feeling, Ruby?"

"Fine."

"No more labor pains?" Ruby shook her head. Dr. Achatz peered at her. "No twinges or aches?" A one-shouldered shrug. Dr. Achatz sighed. "Go ahead and lay back. I'll do an examination to see if you're still dilated."

Ruby glanced over at Page, who asked, "Do you want me to step out or stay with you?"

"Stay."

Ruby reached out her hand, so Page stood and took a spot near Ruby's head, holding the girl's hand. She pushed the girl's bangs back as Dr. Achatz examined her. "You're doing good," she told her even though the girl winced at something the doctor did.

"How do you know?"

"Don't forget I'm a nurse who has been in a lot of these situations." She tried to give her a reassuring smile. "If something was wrong, Dr. Achatz would already have said something."

"She's right, Ruby. Things look good. You're dilated to two but nothing to worry about at this point."

Once the examination was complete, Ruby sat up and Page took a seat next to her on the exam table. Dr. Achatz removed her gloves and placed them in a receptacle. "I don't see anything to be concerned about, but I'd like you to still take it easy. Your blood pressure is slightly elevated, so put your feet up every chance you get. Plenty of water. No caffeine." She wrote something on a prescription pad then tore it off and handed it to Page. "For prenatal vitamins."

Page nodded and put the piece of paper in her shorts pocket. "Thank you, Dr. Achatz."

"Eat several smaller healthy meals rather than three big ones. Based on some of your tests in the hospital, the baby is smaller than it should be at this point." Dr. Achatz put a hand on Ruby's shoulder. "Let's see if we can get some weight on the both of you, okay?"

"Thank you, doctor."

Dr. Achatz pulled out a brochure from the pocket of her lab coat. "I work with a support group that meets at the library for pregnant teens. I thought you might be interested. Our next meeting is tomorrow night."

Ruby accepted the brochure and glanced

at it before handing it to Page. "A support group?"

"It doesn't hurt to talk with others who are going through the same things you are."

Page nodded. "This is a great idea. Thank you again."

Dr. Achatz smiled at them before leaving the room. Ruby slid off the exam table and finished dressing. "So we can go now?"

Page gave a nod. "And you'll hold up your end of the bargain? I've still got this super-wicked craving for ice cream."

"I promised to take you, didn't I?"

Ruby laughed. "You know, you're not supposed to bribe kids into doing the right thing."

"Hey, I'm learning this parent job as we go. Cut me some slack."

Page put an arm around Ruby's shoulders as they walked to the receptionist's window to check out. They made another appointment for two weeks from now, then headed for the parking lot. They drove to Page's favorite ice-cream stand, where she'd once worked. Ruby ogled the long list of flavors. "How am I supposed to pick just one?"

"So pick two."

Ruby grinned and chose honey walnut with chocolate fudge. Page opted for her old favorite, strawberry guava. They took their ice-cream cups to a picnic table and stayed silent while they took their first few bites. Ruby put her mouth around the spoon and closed her eyes. “Good, huh?” Page asked.

“Better than good.”

Page handed her a napkin to wipe the chocolate smear from the side of her lips. “I have to work nights this week, so April said she’d come over and stay with you, okay?”

The spoon stopped halfway to Ruby’s mouth. “I don’t need a babysitter. I’ve been taking care of myself for a while.”

“I know, but I’d feel better knowing that April was there just in case.”

“The doc said I’m fine.”

But Page insisted. “She’s staying over anyway. She’s my best friend, so I’m sure she’ll give you plenty of dirt on me.”

“Ha! You probably got the best grades and was never in trouble.”

“That’s what you think.”

Ruby scoffed. “Please.”

“You think you’re the only one who has run away and lived on the streets?” She hadn't meant to share that, but now it was out there. "We all have a past, Ruby. But what counts is what we do with our present to make a better future." Page paused, then shook her head. "Now I sound like April. Great."

"Why did you run away?"

How much to tell an impressionable girl? Should she tell her about the night that her mother had told her she wished she'd never been born? How it had almost wrecked her life? How Page had let those words sink into her skin until she packed her backpack with clothes and left for school the next morning with the intention of never returning? How she'd slept in her friend's car for over a week until a cop found her and took her home?

Instead, she stared into her ice-cream cup. "Family stuff. With any luck, you'll never meet my mother. She's not exactly the warm-and-fuzzy type." She raised her eyes to Ruby's. "I haven't always been the fierce woman you see before you. I decided I'd be better off alone on the streets than living with her, but the cops didn't agree.

They took me back, and I waited for another chance until I could leave again."

Ruby shook her head, but grinned. "My mom was the best. She had her problems like everybody else, but I never doubted she loved me."

"Then you're lucky and shouldn't forget that." Page pushed her ice cream away, her stomach starting to rebel at the treat. "I should have asked for a smaller scoop."

"You okay?"

Page pasted a smile on her face. "Sure." She took a deep breath and looked around them. "So what do we want to do with the rest of our day?"

"Shouldn't you take a nap or something before you go to work?"

"And here I thought I was the one who was supposed to take care of you and not the other way around."

Ruby shrugged. "Maybe we could take care of each other."

That sounded really good to Page.

April arrived at Page's house after dinner, lugging a tote bag stuffed with teen magazines, cosmetics and snacks for Ruby.

When Page protested, her friend said, "I took a chance and brought what I always wanted when I was her age."

Ruby thanked April profusely and took a seat on the sofa, putting her feet up on the coffee table. Page fought the urge to scold her. The doctor had told her to put her feet up after all. But she wished that she had chosen somewhere else to put them. Maybe they could talk about that tomorrow.

April nudged her. "You okay? Your eyes look all funny, bulging like that."

Page sighed and moved Ruby's feet to the sofa instead. "We don't put our feet on the table here."

Ruby sighed and spoke to April. "She likes her rules, doesn't she?"

"She thrives on them."

Page opened her mouth to protest, but April gave her a wink. "I like things a certain way is all." She adjusted the neckline of her gray scrubs. "Which means no electronics after nine."

Ruby rolled her eyes. "Like I have any electronics."

"That means the TV or my computer."

Page told April, "Make sure she brushes her teeth before bed, too."

"Hey, I'm not five years old."

"And she can read until ten but then lights out."

April gave her a nod. "Any rules you have for me?"

"Don't be a brat." Page grabbed her purse and looked at Ruby, feeling like she was forgetting something. "Are you two going to be okay?"

"Stop worrying. We'll make some popcorn and watch a movie while we do our nails." April waggled her eyebrows at Ruby. "I brought a couple DVDs that I thought you might like."

"Maybe I should get rid of my shifts for this first week with you here?" She should have thought of this before now, but she hadn't expected to feel this strong urge to stay home with Ruby.

She started to pull out her cell phone from her purse, but Ruby stood and nudged Page toward the front door. "We'll be fine. And you don't want to be late for work."

On impulse, Page reached over and kissed Ruby's cheek. "Okay. I'll see you in the morning." She turned to April. "Thank you again."

April waved. "Call me on your break. You'll see everything is just fine."

Page nodded and left before she could change her mind.

THE CELL-PHONE CHIRP woke Page, and she groaned as she rolled over to answer it.

"You're still in bed, Page? I thought I raised you better."

Ugh. Her mother. She should have checked the caller ID before she'd answered. "I work nights. You know that."

"I never know what you're up to. You never call me."

There was a perfectly good reason for that. Some women were born to be loving nurturers. And then there was her mother. Page had worked for years to establish boundaries, mostly to protect herself. But a part of her wondered if her mother would ever change and truly see her for who she was, a person deserving of love, instead of an obligation and a nuisance. "Is there something you wanted?"

"Just checking to see if you'd died yet."

Okay, so maybe she'd always stay the same. "Nope. Not dead. Disappointed?"

"Why do you keep fighting? Just give up already. You've clearly lost the lottery three times, babe. You won't get a fourth chance."

And her mother actually asked why she never called? "Thanks for the pep talk. Gotta go."

"Wait!" Her mother paused on the other end. "You should know that your father is getting married again."

That would make lucky wife number six. "And you think I should call and congratulate him? We don't talk. Ever." She paused. "How old is this one?"

"Old enough to drink, I think."

Her father loved three things: himself, bourbon and young women. Page had long ago given up on him changing. "Can I go now?"

"Try not to die before the holidays. I'd hate to be alone at Christmas."

And then her mother hung up. Page glared at the phone and dropped it on the nightstand. For a few moments she considered how she'd ended up with her parents. That thought made her wonder how she'd gotten cancer three times. She placed her hand on her belly above where her ovary created toxic organisms that she fought hard to keep from taking over the rest of her body.

There was a knock on her bedroom door. "Come in."

Ruby popped her head inside. "I didn't want to wake you, but that guy, Mateo, is here."

Page sat upright in bed and immediately regretted it as her head spun and her stomach revolted. She covered her mouth and ran to the bathroom, hoping to make it in time.

After she cleaned herself up, she threw on a gray T-shirt and black shorts before walking into the living room. Mateo, looking good as always in a navy blue shirt and jeans, sat on the couch. He stood as she entered the room. "I forgot you were working nights."

"I was awake. Is everything okay?" She crossed the room and sat next to him on the sofa.

Ruby started to leave when Mateo turned to her. "You might as well stay. This involves you as well." He pulled a folded piece of paper from his pocket and held it out to Page. "Names and addresses of potential fathers."

Page glanced over at Ruby, whose jaw had dropped. She took the paper and unfolded it, scanning through the information. "So soon?"

He rubbed his palms on his thighs. "There's no guarantee that Ruby's father is on that list, but it gives us a place to start."

Page looked up at him. "Us?"

"I'm all the way in on this one." He gave shrugged. "This is what you're paying me to do."

Right. For a moment, she'd forgotten they weren't more than client and attorney. She tried to push down the disappointment, but her heartbeat didn't slow. Instead, it felt as if it would pound out of her chest and everyone would see her feelings for this man. She cleared her throat and stood to hand Ruby the paper. "Does any of this look familiar?"

Ruby took a seat. "I don't know. My mom said that it was just the two of us forever." Her eyes skimmed the list again. "I wish I knew more. Sorry."

"Don't apologize." Mateo rose and took the list from her. "I'll start the groundwork. Check on dates and history of these men. See if I can find any connection with you."

Page got up as well. "Can I get you some coffee? Or do you have to run off?"

"A cup of coffee would be great. I'm meeting my family for breakfast in—" he checked his watch "—half an hour, but I have some time."

Page walked to the kitchen, and Mateo followed her. She poured coffee into a mug. "Cream and sugar?"

"Black is fine."

She handed him the mug, and their fingers touched briefly. Page felt a spark pass between them, but when she peered at Mateo he acted as if nothing had happened.

"Do you really think one of these Thomas Burns could be her father?"

"I don't know." He tapped his finger against the mug. "Like I said, it's a start. I'll do some digging and let you know what I find out."

"And if he's not one of these men? I just

don't want to get Ruby's hopes up only to have her find out that her father will reject her again."

"I contacted a private investigator in Oklahoma to get some more background on both Ruby and her mom. See if there is any mention of a family member. The more we know, the better it is for our case."

"And following the judge's orders."

"Exactly." He took a sip of coffee. "So how are things going with you two?"

She glanced toward the living room, where Ruby was watching television. "Good, I think. We're still learning about each other."

He nodded. "Sounds promising."

"She is so independent and stubborn." She stared at him when he smirked at her. "What?"

"Sounds like someone else I know."

She returned his grin. "You don't know me well enough to say that."

"Hey, I'm learning more and more about you every time I see you. Really see you." He checked his watch. "I hate to run, but can we talk about this later?"

"Sure." She walked him out to his car

and noticed that Ruby was watching them from the window. "So, I guess it's more waiting until we know what to do next?"

"I'll try to check further into Ruby's background. The best thing you can do is to make sure that she's well taken care of."

"I'm already doing that." She took a few steps back so that he could get in his car. She waved as he pulled out of her driveway, accelerated and disappeared from view.

Similarly, Ruby had disappeared from the front window, Page noticed. She sincerely hoped that they wouldn't be setting the girl up for more disappointment.

THE CROWD INSIDE the diner swelled with the Saturday-morning breakfast crowd. Mateo scanned the place, looking for his sister and brother-in-law. Lulu waved from a table near the back. He squeezed between tables and chairs, moving in her direction. He took a seat next to his dad and turned over a ceramic mug as a waitress passed by with a coffee carafe. "You had to pick the busiest spot to meet?"

After the waitress filled Mateo's mug, Lulu waved off a second cup, but Roberto and his dad slid their mugs over for refills. "I figured we would be safe meeting at ten and the breakfast rush would be over. Speaking of which, you're late."

"Had to give a client an update on something I'm working on." He blew across the mug before taking a sip of coffee.

"And you couldn't have done that over the phone?" she asked.

He could have, but he'd woken up with a need to see Page. He was curious to know more about her. What she thought about… everything, really. Before he could change his mind, he'd found himself sitting in his car in front of her address. "Her house is on the way here, so it was no big deal."

Lulu's eyes widened. "*Her?* Is she young and single?"

Roberto groaned and his father chuckled. "Now you've done it. She's going to have you married off to this client within a month. Watch."

Mateo stopped the conversation by opening his menu and hiding behind it before his sister could get anything from him. But she pushed down the edge of the menu. "You're talking about Page."

"How do you know her?" He narrowed his eyes, then cocked his head to one side. "The aunties have been talking."

"I think it's their job to discuss our business amongst themselves. And since Sherri and I both got married, you're one of the last for them to play matchmaker with." She clapped her hands. "This is going to be fun."

"No, it's not. There's nothing romantic between Page and myself." And maybe if he said it enough times, he could start believing that this sudden urge to see her was nothing. Even if the hope that had flared in her eyes when he'd handed her the Thomas Burns list had made him want to do more for her. He wanted to put more hope in those hazel-green eyes. Wanted to make her smile. He rubbed his face. What was happening to him?

The waitress returned to take their orders. Once she left, Lulu took her husband's hand and looked across the table. "Roberto and I have some big news."

His dad took a deep breath and held it. He clasped his hands and brought them up to his face. "You're...?"

Lulu nodded and started to cry. “Pregnant.”

His dad gave a shout and jumped up to embrace his daughter. “I’m so happy, *mija*.”

Mateo stood and shook Roberto’s hand, then took his turn hugging his little sister. “I thought you said you were waiting.”

Roberto gave a sheepish grin. “That was the plan, but this one had other ideas.” He put an arm around Lulu and drew her close to his side. “We’re due beginning of next year.”

Lulu looked at their father. “February twenty-fifth.”

His mother’s birthday. A wave of loss swept through Mateo, and he closed his eyes. “That’s… Wow. Just…wow.”

His dad wiped at his eyes. “She would have loved to be here. So proud of the young woman you’ve become, Lu.”

“I wish she was here.” Lulu grabbed her napkin and dabbed at her own tears. “I’m excited and scared and thrilled and… I need her.”

“We’ll be there for you. Whatever you need.” Mateo reached across the table and held her hand. “How are you feeling?”

She grinned and crumpled the napkin. "Okay, I guess. I don't know. I'm still trying to process all of this."

His father held up his mug. "I think this calls for a toast. To Roberto and my precious Lulu. May you be blessed with a healthy and happy baby."

They clinked mugs and shared smiles.

PAGE PULLED UP in front of the library and turned to look at Ruby, who was staring out the windshield. "This is a library? It's huge."

"They hold a lot of meetings and community activities here. Like the support group. Let's go." Page got out and Ruby followed her inside the building. "The pamphlet says they meet on the second floor. Stairs or elevator?"

Ruby put a hand on her belly. "Elevator. I'm trying to take it easy."

"Good answer."

They found the elevator and took it to the second floor. The hushed atmosphere made them drop the volume on their voices as well as they walked the long hallway to the indicated meeting room. Page started to walk in, but Ruby grabbed her arm. "Wait."

Page raised an eyebrow. "What's wrong?"

Ruby leaned against the wall and looked up at the ceiling. "Nerves."

"Remember, everyone is in a similar situation to yours. They might have some good advice. You have to see the bigger picture." Page put a hand on the teen's shoulder. "I belong to a cancer support group myself. Don't tell April, but the meetings really do help. I don't feel so alone in my battle."

"Fine. I'll give it a try." Ruby started to walk into the room, then turned and held up a finger to Page. "One meeting."

Page smirked. This sounded very similar to what she'd told April when she'd first visited Hope Center. It had been almost four years now since that first meeting, and the only ones she missed were when she had to work a shift at the hospital. "Agreed."

A woman about Page's mother's age approached them as they entered. "Welcome. I'm Ranjan, the counselor who runs the group. I'm glad to see you here. How did you find out about our meeting?"

Ruby glanced at the other young women,

who chatted with each other, her eyes darting around the room.

Page smiled at the counselor. “Dr. Achatz recommended it.”

“Angela has been a wonderful supporter of ours.” She turned to Ruby. “Dear, would you like to take a seat?”

Ruby looked at Page. “I’ll see you later?” She walked away and approached a teenager who was sitting alone.

“And you are her…”

“Guardian.”

“We usually meet for two hours, depending on how the conversation goes.” Ranjan walked Page to the door. “She’s one of our younger members, but she’ll be fine.”

“Thank you. I’ll be back to pick her up.” Page gave a small wave to Ruby, but Ruby was talking to her new acquaintance and didn’t see it.

Page exited the library. The summer evening left her free and at loose ends, wanting some company. She pulled out her cell phone and dialed April, but it went to voice mail. She hung up and dialed another number. Mateo picked up on the third ring. “Page?”

"Are you free to meet for coffee? I have some questions."

He paused on the other end. "Sure, but I'd rather go for a walk if you're up for it."

"The River Walk?"

"Give me ten minutes."

She drove to the downtown park area and waited until she saw Mateo arrive. She walked toward his car. "Thank you for meeting with me."

He gave a shrug. "I was tired of reading briefs on such a beautiful night. I'm grateful for the break."

He motioned for her to go first. They walked toward the Detroit River on the boardwalk. "You said you have some questions."

She gave a shrug. "It was an excuse to see you."

He stopped walking, and she did the same, wanting to see the expression on his face. "Page…"

"You said you wanted to be friends, but anytime I see you it's with Ruby there. I thought we could spend some time alone."

That seemed to appease him as he started walking again. "Speaking of Ruby…"

"She's at a support-group meeting for teen pregnancy."

He nodded, approving. "That will be good for her."

"Can we talk about something besides Ruby?"

"What do you want to talk about?"

Page took a few steps then paused to lean against the railing that separated the walk from the river. He stood beside her, bending to rest his arms on the railing. "Did you ever picture your life like this? That is where you would be now?"

"Wow. You're diving in deep."

"I'm serious." She turned to him. "I thought I'd be happily married with kids. The perfect mom with the perfect life."

"What's wrong with your life now?"

"No husband, no kids. Fighting cancer." She shook her head. "Not exactly the happy ending they write books about."

"Do you want me to tell you what I see? You're a strong woman who has beat the odds more than once. You became the guardian for a pregnant teen when she had no one else and needed you. You're a good friend to my cousin, who would have been lost without your support when she was fighting cancer." He reached out and caressed her cheek. "I see an amazing woman whom I've come to admire a lot."

She dropped her gaze to his mouth. The moment was broken, though, when she heard someone calling his name. Another couple approached them. Mateo lit up and hugged the petite woman who resembled him. "What are you doing here, Lulu?"

"I could ask you the same thing." The woman held out a hand to Page. "I'm Mateo's sister, and this is my husband, Roberto."

Page shook hands with both of them. "Page."

"Ah, the client." Lulu pretended to punch Mateo in the shoulder. "You never mentioned she was so pretty."

Page could feel her cheeks grow warm. "Thank you."

Roberto cleared his throat. "We didn't mean to interrupt you two."

"Yes, it looked as if you were discussing something very important." Lulu grinned. "It was nice to meet you, Page. I'm sure I'll be hearing more about you. We will be talking about this later, right, Mateo?"

"Please stop." His words didn't sound angry, but amused. When the couple left, he turned to Page. "Sorry. My sister likes to play matchmaker. I hope she didn't embarrass you as much as she did me."

"It's fine."

Mateo motioned that they should continuing walking, so they did, heading farther down the boardwalk. "Where were we?"

He'd been touching her cheek, and she'd been wondering if he was about to kiss her. "You said you admire me."

He glanced at her briefly. "I do. But to answer your first question—no, my life isn't what I pictured, either."

"What did you expect?"

"That I'd be a successful lawyer who drove a fancy car. Maybe married."

"You don't think you're successful?"

He gave a wry snicker. "My clients lately have been getting younger and in more trouble than I'm happy with. I don't know how much longer I can do this."

"What if you're their only hope?"

"Page..."

"You were Ruby's. And mine. And just maybe, you do help them, no matter what their sentence is."

"You can't know that."

"Sherri told me you were the best lawyer because you actually cared about your clients. That you didn't take a case just for the money. Because you believed that you could help your client with whatever situation they were in." She reached out and took his hand. "Don't give up on that, Mateo."

"It's not that simple."

"Why can't it be? Maybe I admire you, too, because I believe you make a difference. And we need more people like that."

They looked at each other for a long moment, then Mateo glanced at his watch. "I need to get back to preparing a case."

Disappointed that their time was getting cut short, Page nodded. "I have to go pick up Ruby."

In silence, they walked back to their cars.

Before she had a chance to say goodbye, Mateo spoke. "I appreciate what you said, but I'm burned out. Nice words won't change that."

She could easily see the pain in his eyes. "That's too bad. You really are a good lawyer."

He walked away, his head down. She wished she could have lightened his burden, as he had for her.

Whenever she thought they were taking a step toward each other, something made it feel as if they were actually taking two steps apart. Would their timing ever be right?

IT BOTHERED MATEO all evening the way he'd left things with Page earlier. Unable to stand it a moment longer, he called her. "Page? I never thanked you for the walk earlier. It was nice. Helped me clear my head a bit. How was Ruby's meeting?"

"She said it was okay. Her favorite part was when the counselor brought out cookies at the end."

Silence on both ends until he cleared his throat. "I've been thinking about what you said."

"I've been thinking about your words, too."

"I meant them."

"So did I."

He leaned against his headboard and gripped the cell phone. "I appreciate you trying to encourage me, but it's complicated."

"I just thought you shouldn't give up on something that's so important."

"I get that. And I haven't given up completely. I need to change my focus."

"Well, I hope you find what you're looking for."

He smiled. "Thanks. You, too."

They said their goodbyes, but he still had her in his thoughts long after they hung up.

PAGE AND RUBY arrived at Hope Center and found a parking spot nearby so that Page could leave early for work. "April will take you home after the meeting. Okay, Ruby?"

Ruby seemed focused on the storefront, where various colored ribbons decorated the available space. "What did you say this place was again?"

"Hope Center. Cancer support groups. Similar to the one you went to the other night."

"Right." Ruby wrinkled her nose. "I told you I'd stay home and watch TV."

Page squelched a grin. "I understand the feeling, believe me. I acted the same way when April brought me to my first meeting. She had to drag me practically kicking and screaming."

"And you brought me because..."

"If I have to be tortured, then you do, too, kiddo." She laughed at Ruby's horrified expression. "Joking. I'd just feel better knowing you're not home by yourself." She held up a hand as the girl started to protest. "I know you can take care of yourself, okay? So call me overprotective, if you want to, however, I'm sure you'll appreciate having someone with you for now and to make sure that everything is okay."

Ruby huffed and got out of the car.

So maybe she could let up a little with the hovering, but until they knew Ruby and the baby were out of the woods, Page would insist on not leaving her charge alone.

Together, they entered the center. April waved them over. "I saved these two chairs for you."

Ruby took a seat while Page checked in

at the table and wrote out name tags for them. She returned to the circle of metal folding chairs and handed a sticker to Ruby. "They like knowing our names."

"Why do I have to wear one? Not like they're going to be talking to me." But she removed the paper backing from the tag and stuck it to the front of her T-shirt.

April put an arm around the girl. "You never know what's going to happen at one of these meetings. We could all end up with our arms around each other singing songs."

Ruby's head snapped toward Page, her eyes wide. Page laughed. "Don't worry. We don't make you join in the singing until the second meeting."

Her friend Sherri leaned over and held out her hand to Ruby. "I'm Sherri. I've heard a lot about you, Ruby."

April grinned. "I might have told her how we had a face-off on musical trivia. And that I won."

"There's no way you won. I recited the last eight years of Tony winners."

"But I could name all the Sondheim musicals," April countered.

Page held her hands up in the formation

of a T. "I thought we agreed you were both musical divas."

Ruby crossed her arms and leaned back into her chair. "Some of us more than others."

Lynn, the support group leader, walked to the center of the circle and swept her gaze around to each member present. "We'll get started in a moment. I understand Page has brought a special visitor. Would you like to introduce her, Page?"

Page stood and said, "This is Ruby, who will be staying with me for a while." She sat down quickly.

April looked over at her. "That's all you're going to say?"

"If Ruby wants to share more information, I'll let her do it."

April whispered to Ruby, "She doesn't like sharing much in circle time."

"I share plenty," Page replied. A few of the members mumbled responses to this, and Page narrowed her eyes. "I first talked about my divorce here. And when the cancer came back."

Lynn walked over to her and put a hand on her shoulder. "We know how difficult talking about yourself can be. Maybe it was because your mother made herself the focus when you were growing up."

"Whoa." Page looked around the room. "When did I become the topic of the night?"

"All I'm saying is that how we were raised tends to influence who we become." Lynn glanced at the rest of the support group. "In fact, I'm changing what I was going to talk about. Let's discuss our families and their role in our recovery. Would you like to start, Page?"

"No. Because there's nothing I have to share."

April leaned forward. "You know you'll feel better once you get it off your chest." When Page didn't respond, her friend sighed. "Fine. I'll go. My family was amazing. Once we learned it was cancer, my mom moved down here to take care of me even though her life is four hours away."

Sherri nodded. "Mine moved in, too."

Other women started to share how their families had stepped up after their cancer diagnoses. They told about meals cooked and heads shaved and a thousand things that Page had never had. When she'd told her parents the first time, they acted as they always did, and had ignored her and her needs. No offers of driving her to chemo. No words of encouragement. Nothing. But then they'd never been involved in her life before. Why would cancer change that?

"We were blessed with great families." April reached over and took Page's hand. "But I've also been blessed with a best friend who is just as close as a sister. I don't think family means just the one we're born into. It includes those we bring into our circle and I wouldn't trade a million blood relatives for you, Page."

Page sniffed and squeezed April's hand. "I couldn't ask for a better friend. You've always been there for me."

"And I always will be."

Page joined in now. "If my parents have done anything, it's to show me about how I don't want to live. I want to be involved in my child's life, if I ever get lucky enough to become a mom. For now, though, it means being a foster parent to Ruby. That's why I brought you tonight. Why I'm overprotective. I don't want you to ever think that I don't want you to be in my life."

The girl blinked back at her, a single tear making a jagged track down her cheek. Ruby swallowed and gave a short nod, then stood and walked out of the meeting. Page raised an eyebrow at April, who pointed to the door.

Page excused herself and walked outside to find Ruby clasping her belly and crying. She jogged up to the girl. “Are you okay? Is it the baby?”

Ruby raised her eyes to Page’s. “I’m okay.”

“Then what’s wrong?”

“What you said in there?” Ruby wiped at her wet face. “You mean all that?”

“I care about you, kid.”

Ruby nodded, and the tears came faster.

“Hey, I didn’t mean to make you cry.”

“Maybe it’s hormones.” The girl dropped her gaze. “Or maybe it’s because no one’s cared about me since my mom died. And I really, really miss her.”

Page pulled Ruby into a hug. “I know you do.” She rubbed the girl’s back until her sobs quieted. “It’ll get easier with time. I promise.”

“Doesn’t seem like it.”

"You're never going to forget your mom, but it won't hurt as much when you think about her as time goes by. You'll remember the good times and they'll make you smile." She rested her cheek against the girl's forehead. "And soon you'll be a mom yourself."

Ruby backed away, keeping her eyes on the ground. "No. I've decided to let someone adopt the baby."

Page had wondered a lot about how Ruby was going to handle things. It was probably for the best. "If that's what you want."

Ruby looked up into Page's face. "It is. And I want you to be the one to do the adopting."

CHAPTER SIX

DR. ACHATZ CLEARED her throat and snapped her fingers at Page. "Are you with us?"

Page blinked and shook her head to clear the cobwebs. "Sorry. I wish I could say it was chemo brain, but I've got something on my mind." She double-checked the tray of instruments and saw that everything was there. "Once they bring in your patient, I'll be fine."

"Good. Because I need you to be focused on this." Dr. Achatz turned as the OR doors opened and the expectant mother arrived, sitting on a gurney and clutching her belly. "Amanda, are you ready to meet your daughter?"

The patient nodded and Dr. Achatz started giving orders to her staff. Page concentrated on handing the instruments as they were called for and following the doctor's directions. When the baby slipped from her mother's body, Page had to blink the tears away as she performed all the necessary checks and cleaned her off and carried her to the parents.

It had been a routine delivery, but it had felt different. Full of more mystery and awe somehow. Could it have been Ruby's request that she adopt her baby that had changed things? Page had to admit that she'd been preoccupied by it ever since she'd asked.

She smiled, but shook her head. Was she really considering this? Adopting Ruby's baby and becoming a single mother? Could she do it? Would she?

The new mom and baby were soon sent to the maternity wing. Page started to reset the OR, checking and counting each instrument, sponge and roll of gauze. Dr. Achatz approached her. "Would you mind telling me what's distracting you?"

Page winced. "I'm not sure."

Dr. Achatz gave her a look that told her that she didn't believe her. "Somehow I don't think it's the midwife program we've been talking about."

If she did adopt the baby, her college

plans would have to be put on hold. She doubted she could work, go to school and take care of a baby. She was already finding it difficult to juggle Ruby and her job. And the teenager could take care of herself for the most part. "I got a strange request that came out of the blue and my mind has been considering all the scenarios ever since."

"How strange?"

"My foster daughter asked me to adopt her baby."

Dr. Achatz stopped scrubbing her hands and left the water running, and she faced Page. "Wow. Did you know that she was thinking about that?"

"I honestly didn't know what she was planning to do about the baby until she asked me." She handed Dr. Achatz a towel to dry her hands. "I figured that I'd never be a mom after all I've been through. But now? It's like a different future is dangling in front of me, one I'd given up on. It's a lot to think about."

"She's six months along, right? You've got time to consider it."

"And so does she. What if I agree and she changes her mind? Or what if, because of my cancer, I can't adopt?" Page took a deep breath. "I'm getting ahead of myself, aren't I?"

Dr. Achatz nodded. "What you should do is contact a good family lawyer."

Page allowed a grin to grace her face. "Just so happens I know the best."

MATEO BALANCED HIS cup of coffee, briefcase and office keys as he opened the door to his law office. Then someone was taking the coffee before it tipped and spilled down his front. He turned to thank the Good Samaritan and stared into Page's stormy green eyes. "Thanks."

She gave a nod and followed him into the office. He placed his briefcase on the desk and she put his coffee next to it. "I just happened to be in the right place at the right time."

"Good thing you were." He shrugged out of his suit coat and draped it over his chair. "Did we have an appointment?"

"Actually, I got off work early and drove right here. I wanted to discuss a legal question with you."

"About Ruby?"

She took a seat across from him. "What are my chances of being able to adopt her baby?"

Mateo took a deep breath and considered her. "I didn't expect that question."

"Believe me, this wasn't part of our original plan. She sprung it on me last night." She sat back in the chair and crossed her arms over her belly. "I was approved as a foster mother, so it wouldn't take much more, right?"

"A *temporary* foster parent. And of a *teenager* still years away from being an adult." Mateo tapped his fingers against his lips. "A single, adoptive mother fighting cancer? In midtreatment? I don't know, Page. I don't want to get your hopes up, but it sounds like an uphill battle."

"But you're not saying it's impossible? Look what happened with Ruby. You thought the cancer would preclude me from that, too."

He looked across the desk at her and doubted the word *impossible* was part of her vocabulary. She seemed to be the kind of woman who would take on any type of challenge and wouldn't take no for an answer. That kind of attitude could help. "I'll make a search for a precedent that will back up your case." He leaned forward. "Are you sure that you want to take this on? I don't mean caring for the baby, but the court battle we could face."

"I've wanted to be a mother since I can remember. And I thought that cancer had taken that away from me. But now, there's this door that's opened, and I don't want to walk by it without finding out if I can have what I've always wanted."

"Okay. I'll look into it."

Page stood and extended her hand to him. "Deal."

He put his hand in hers, covering it with his other. He watched her intently for a moment. "It's not going to be easy," he said.

"Story of my life." She grabbed her purse and slung it over her shoulder. "I should go home and try to get some sleep. I'll be glad when these night shifts are done." She started to leave the office, but paused in the doorway. "April said they invited you to the wedding. Are you going?"

"That was the plan."

"Are you taking a date?"

He hadn't even considered it. There wasn't anyone he could think of to ask except for the woman before him. And she was off-limits. Not only was she a client, but he also still didn't want to get involved with someone whose life was so fragile. He had moments when he thought about a relationship with Page, but in the end he couldn't. "No. You?"

She shook her head. "Maybe you'll save a dance for me?"

That he could do. "Sounds like a plan."

She smiled and left the office. Mateo started his computer, waited for it to load his programs. He glanced at the door through which Page had disappeared. For someone he'd sworn not to get involved with, the more time he was in her presence, the more he grew to admire her spunk and grit. She was no pushover or victim. Yes, she might have cancer, but she wasn't going to let it stop her from following her dreams.

But then he'd once thought that about his mother.

With his computer booted up, he brought up a law search engine. He wouldn't be more for her than her lawyer, but he could do the best job he could and help her get what she wanted.

THE ALARM SOUNDED and Page removed the eye mask and winced at the light that streamed through the closed blinds. She shut off the alarm, got out of bed and went to check on Ruby. She opened her bedroom door. "Ruby?"

The teenager sat on the sofa and was watching television while eating from a bag of chips. She sat up and brushed crumbs from her belly. "Was the TV too loud? I could turn it down."

"It's fine." She took a seat next to Ruby and helped herself to some chips. "What are you watching?"

"Don't know. I was flipping channels. You should go back to sleep."

"I don't want to sleep the whole day away. Besides, I have tonight off and can go to bed early." Page peered at her foster daughter. "How are you feeling?"

Ruby shrugged. "Okay, I guess. No pains if that's what you mean."

"Did you take your vitamins?"

She rolled her eyes. "Yes."

Page held up the bag of chips. "And what have you eaten besides these?"

"PB and J. And a banana."

"Maybe we should go to the fruit market and get you some fresh produce. You want to be sure you're eating the right things for the baby." Page knew she should get off the sofa and take them to the store, but the idea of going anywhere made her more tired.

Ruby looked over at her. "Have you thought about what I asked?"

She'd done little else. "You know I have cancer. And while I'm still in treatment, my chances of survival are questionable."

Ruby shifted on her end of the sofa. "So you don't want the baby?"

Page put a hand to her chest. "I do. And I talked to Mateo to find out if a judge would grant me the adoption based on my condition. But he thinks it could be a tough sell."

Ruby gave a huge sigh. "But what if that's what I want and you want? Doesn't that count for anything?"

"It will certainly help. But let's not think about that right now. We'll let Mateo do his job, meanwhile, we'll concentrate on making sure you stay healthy and happy."

"Happy?" Ruby gave a derisive chuckle. "I'm not sure what that would look like."

Page sat up straighter. Happiness seemed to be as elusive to Ruby as it was for herself. "What do you want to do after the baby's born? Have you thought about your future?"

"Go back to school. Get my diploma, I guess. Maybe college." Ruby rubbed her belly. "When my mom died and I got pregnant, I stopped thinking about tomorrow. Only focused on the day ahead of me. How to find food to eat. A place to stay. I guess I had an idea of finding my dad, which is why I'm in Detroit." She stopped and rested. "Do girls like me get a future?"

"Of course you do. And I'll do whatever I can to make sure of it."

"Why?"

"Because you deserve it."

Ruby smiled and took Page's hand and placed it where she could feel the baby moving. "That's amazing. The baby's pretty active."

"The doctor asked me if I wanted to

know the sex of the baby, but I didn't then." Ruby raised her eyes to Page's. "Would you want to know?"

Once upon a time when she was still married to Chad, she'd imagined leaving their baby's gender to be a surprise. But then, she wasn't a big fan of surprises, either. "I don't think I would." Page closed her eyes for a moment. "I have some good news and bad news. Which do you want first?"

Ruby screwed her mouth to the side. "Give me the good news first."

"I'm not working nights anymore. In fact, I'm taking some time off. A few days. The bad news is that I go for my next chemo treatment tomorrow, so I'll be spending a lot of time sleeping."

Ruby brightened at this. "I can take care of you. I know how to make soup and toast and stuff. I'll bring you blankets and magazines and whatever you need. I promise."

"I'd appreciate that. Hopefully this time won't be so bad." She rested her head on the back of the sofa. It would be nice to have someone take care of her. "And then I have

April's wedding coming up soon after that. Hopefully I'll be feeling better by then."

"She invited me. Did she tell you?"

That sounded like something April would do. In fact, April's fiancé, Zach, had told her she had to stop inviting random people to the wedding since the banquet hall only held so many. April was generous to a fault, though, and kept adding more guests.

"We'll have to find you something to wear."

Ruby shuddered. "More shopping?"

Page shuddered, too. "They have a lot of choices online, so fingers crossed we can order something and get it here by then."

"I love the way you think."

MATEO HUNG UP the phone and crossed another name off the list of Ruby's potential fathers. Out of almost two dozen possibilities, twenty names had been eliminated. He'd finally gotten a copy of Ruby's birth certificate that morning and it had helped him in the search. Ruby's mother had included Thomas's middle initial, which helped Mateo narrow the search.

He entered the next name and vital statistics into the online search engine and got a phone number. He dialed it, but an incessant beeping told him the phone number was no longer valid. He put a question mark by that name and moved on.

A knock on the door interrupted his work. He closed the file on his desk, rose and opened the door to find a young woman standing there. “Mr. Lopez, I wasn’t sure if you’d be in today.”

“We don’t have an appointment.”

“Your sister said you wouldn’t mind.”

Mateo waved her inside. “Lulu recommended me?” He’d have to remind his sister to give him advance warning the next time she told a friend about his practice. “How can I help you?”

The young woman took a seat, and Mateo walked behind the desk and pushed his chair back before sitting. Despite the heat of the August day, the woman wore a long-sleeved blouse and dark pants. Her gaze tipped down. Was she hiding something? Finally, she looked up at him and tugged one sleeve past her wrist. “I need to leave my husband.”

“You’re seeking a divorce.”

"Lulu said you take this kind of case."

"I do. Are there any children in the marriage?"

The woman shook her head vigorously. "No, I lost the last pregnancy."

Based on her behavior, he wondered if there were more serious issues going on here. "I'll get the paperwork started. Do you have somewhere safe where you can go once he's served the summons?"

The woman looked shocked and was about to say something, but changed her mind. A minute passed, maybe two, before she said, "My sister's. She said I could stay with her."

"Good."

He pulled up a file with the necessary papers and asked her questions to complete them. When Mateo told her that Michigan was a no-fault-divorce state, she looked up and glared at him. "He knows what he did. It's his fault."

"The court will ask if there's any possibility of reconciliation."

"I'm never going back."

Mateo nodded and printed off the forms for her signature. "I'll get these sent to the county court office. You're sure you don't want to ask for spousal support?"

"I can take care of myself." Her eyes flashed with a determination that made him think she would be okay after this.

They discussed payment terms—she'd have to pay him in installments, since she was only newly back in the workforce. They shook hands, and he walked her to the door. "If you need anything, Mrs. Stanhope, my number is on your copies of the paperwork. I'll keep in touch as we go along in the process. And if your husband tries anything with you, call the police and then me."

She looked him in his eye. "He wouldn't dare."

She left and Mateo sat at his desk, mulling over the young woman's case. When he had thought about expanding into family law, he thought he could avoid the emotional drain that his juvenile crime cases had been. But listening to her story and knowing how these cases often turned out, he still felt depressed.

Was there no hope in the law? Did it only bring pain or could Mateo find a way to bring redemption somehow? He so wanted to make a difference, but it seemed even more hopeless. He forced himself to return to the next Thomas Burns on his list.

RUBY ACCOMPANIED PAGE to her chemotherapy appointment and watched with wide eyes as the nurse connected the IV to the port near her clavicle that would deliver the poisons to her body. Page handed her a magazine in an attempt to distract her.

Once the infusion began, the nurse left and Page opened her book to the part she'd left off at. The thick melodramatic novel had gotten her through her last round of chemo and would help her now. It was easy to get lost in the story and forget what was happening to her.

Ruby set aside the magazine and took a walk around the large room, stopping at the window that overlooked the parking lot. Then she strolled past the other chemo patients and returned to her seat next to Page. "I'm bored."

Page knew the feeling, but she didn't have a choice of whether she wanted to be here or not. "The chair isn't very comfortable for you?"

"No." She picked up the magazine, flipped through it. "How long do we have to be here?"

"At least six hours." She put the marker into her book and placed it beside her. "Would you rather talk?"

"No." Ruby scooted down in the chair and let out another big sigh. "Adults like to talk too much."

Page tried to squelch a grin. "How was your meeting last night?"

"I told them how I asked you to adopt my baby. The counselor seemed surprised."

"Why surprised?"

"Like you said, the cancer thing might stop our plan." She shifted in the chair. "We have to make it work, though."

"We will." Page hoped they could, but she couldn't show any uncertainty with Ruby.

"We also talked about being pregnant and going to school. And alternatives."

"Alternatives?"

"Ranjan said there's a school I could go to and not feel out of place."

"Are you interested?"

"I could be."

Page nodded. “Education is very important. It’s what helped me get out of my home and take care of myself.”

“Did you always know you wanted to be a nurse?”

“I didn’t know what I wanted to be. In high school, I got a part-time job at the hospital in the cafeteria because I could get free food during work. I’d deliver meals to patients, and I saw how nurses helped them. I found myself wanting to do that, too. To help people get better. So I graduated high school and worked as a nurse’s aide while I attended nursing school.”

“How did you start with the babies?”

“I was working in the ER, and a woman arrived in labor. I assisted April with the delivery, and it was amazing.” She smiled at the memory. “I’ve never thought about being anything since.”

“I wish I knew what I wanted to do like you.”

“You’re still young, Ruby. Concentrate on graduating high school first. You have time to figure it out.”

Ruby nodded and looked at the IV. “Does it hurt?”

Page shook her head. “Not anymore. I’m used to it.”

“How many times do you have to do this?”

“This is my fourth one this time round. Last time, I had eight before surgery, and they’ll test me after the sixth infusion now to make sure the cancer is gone.” Hopefully for good.

“What does it feel like?”

Page reached to the port underneath her skin near her shoulder. “This one burns a little. The next one feels like warm honey. But everyone reacts differently.”

“And do you get really sick?”

“I’m on some pretty strong stuff, so yes. Probably tomorrow night it will get worse, but then each day gets better.”

“I can’t imagine letting them do that to me.”

“The alternative is worse.” Page tried to smile. “I’m fighting with everything I’ve got, so I’ll let them pump this poison into my system. Cancer doesn’t stand a chance with me.”

Ruby shrugged. “I thought this was your third time.”

"It is, but I'm determined to make sure it's also the last." Page reached over and took Ruby's hand in her own. "You're not worried about me, are you?"

Ruby looked at the other patients. Page could only guess what she was thinking. Six years before on her first chemo treatment, she had watched the others and compared herself. She wasn't as bad as this person, but someone else was doing better than herself. She'd tried to determine the success of her treatment based on those she saw in that room.

The problem with cancer was that it wasn't predictable. Some of those she figured were doing better had died, while those who seemed to be worse off had beaten it. And she was back for the third time. So, what did that say about her?

"I'm thirsty."

Page turned her attention back to Ruby. "I've got bottles of water in my bag here. And if you get hungry, I packed some granola bars and fruit." Ruby made a face, and Page laughed at it. "It's what I can handle on chemo days. If you hand me my wallet, I'll give you money for the cafeteria."

Ruby took several bills, asked if she wanted something and left. A moment later, April entered the room and spotted Page. She claimed Ruby's vacated chair. "Where's Ruby?"

"She wanted something better than water to drink. But my guess is that she's buying good, old-fashioned junk food downstairs."

"She's fourteen. What else would you expect?"

"True." Page looked her friend over. "You're a little more than a week away from the wedding. Are you ready?"

"Seems like every time I scratch one item off my to-do list, three more get added." April smiled despite her frustrated tone. "Zach threatened to whisk me away to elope, but he knows that we've put too much work into this wedding. Besides, his assistant, Dalvin, wouldn't tolerate his contribution going down the drain."

Page smirked at this, remembering the daily emails that Dalvin had been sending to her about what she needed to do as maid of honor. Then again, he'd kept her on task, and she'd started to look forward to reading those reminders. "You'll be glad of everything he's done once it's over. Have you two planned the honeymoon?"

April let out a big sigh and settled back into the chair, a dreamy smile on her face. "Marking off another item on our second-chance list. We're going to eat our way through Italy. Try the food in each region. I'll be coming home fat and happy."

"That sounds like a wonderful idea." Page winced as a hot prickle moved down her arm. She turned and adjusted the IV tube, finding a kink and straightening it. "I'm so jealous of the two of you."

"You'll get your turn soon enough."

Page grunted. "I'll just be satisfied to get through my treatment and be cancer-free. The whole guy and wedding thing can wait."

"I don't know. Seems like you and Mateo are getting pretty friendly." She waggled her eyebrows and grinned at her.

"That's because of the whole adoption case. Trust me. He's not interested. He knows what he wants. Or doesn't want, in my case. It's fine."

"I think you're fooling yourself, but then I never figured that I'd be marrying Zach."

She fiddled with her engagement ring. “And now, I can’t imagine a life without him.”

“Everything works out for you. You’re like one of those fairy-tale princesses.”

“And you’re who, the cute sidekick? You could be a princess, if you wanted to be.”

Page couldn’t imagine herself in a tiara, so she’d pass on that. “The happily-ever-after can happen to you, but not for me.”

“Maybe your version of a happy ending looks different than mine.” April scooted closer to Page. “Maybe you get the baby before the husband.”

Page sighed. “Getting the baby might not even happen. Mateo warned me it’s going to be tough. And the result might not go in my favor.”

“So you’re giving up already?” April frowned at her. “I thought you were past all this negative thinking.”

“No, you’re past it. I’m still in the middle of it.” Page gestured to her IV. “Look where I am. I’m fighting and hoping, but it could all be for nothing. And the adoption could go the same way.”

April raised an eyebrow at her. “Are you finished?”

Page glared at her. “Don’t do that. Don’t discount my worries like they’re nothing.”

“That’s because that’s exactly what they are right now. Nothing. You don’t have a crystal ball any more than I do. You can’t know how things are going to turn out.”

“And neither do you.”

April bit her lip. “You’re right. I don’t know. But what I do know is that you like to give up before anything happens. I won’t let you do that again. Not with the cancer. And not with this baby.”

Page stewed over April’s words. It’s not like she always expected the worst. Or even if she did expect it, she still hoped for the best. But she always fell back on how her life had turned out so far. So far having her dreams become a reality wasn’t a part of that. With Chad, she’d thought that she’d finally gotten what she’d always wanted. But then he’d cheated on her and divorced her and the cancer came back. She closed her eyes and took a deep breath. Could she take a chance and hope that it all would work out?

And while she was at it, maybe she could hope that Mateo would change his mind and see her as a desirable woman rather than a bald cancer victim. Lately, he seemed more open about things, maybe that included her as well.

When she opened her eyes, she saw that April had tears tracking down both cheeks. Page reached out and wiped them away with her fingers. "I'm trying, April. I really am. I want all of it, but what if it doesn't happen for me?"

April grabbed her hands and squeezed them tight. "I wish you could see how lucky you really are." When Page started to protest, April cut her off. "I mean, how many women do you know that get diagnosed with cancer the third time and still stand up and fight? You are a strong, amazing woman. My best friend in the whole world. And despite what you think, you deserve to get what you want. To be happy and whole."

Page stared at her friend, not knowing what to say. Instead, she leaned forward and hugged her tightly. "Thank you."

MATEO HAD CALLED PAGE, saying that he would stop by after work to give both her and Ruby an update on the father search. He pulled into the driveway behind Page's car and paused. He could have done this over the phone, but he had wanted to see her. He couldn't say why, but being in Page's presence had become important. And he figured he could bring them dinner.

He got out of the car with two bags of food from his uncle's restaurant and walked up to the porch. Before he could knock, the screen door opened and Ruby looked out at him. "She's not feeling so good, Mr. Lopez."

"Should I come back tomorrow?"

"I don't think it would be any better then. She said she might feel worse." She stepped back so that he could enter. "But if you got bad news, then maybe you should tell her next week."

He followed Ruby. A black-and-white quilt was draped over the sofa along with two pillows. He saw a glass of water and bottle of ginger ale on the coffee table along with a cellophane sleeve of saltine crackers. He figured this was evidence of a recent chemo treatment. Maybe he didn't need to see Page so badly.

"Hey, Mateo." Page entered the living

room and made it over to her spot on the sofa.

He held up the bags. "I brought dinner, but it doesn't look like you'd be interested."

She shook her head. "What news did you have for us?"

She looked much as he remembered his mother after one of her infusions. The gaunt, pale look. Hollow cheeks. Dull eyes. He placed the bags of food on the coffee table, then took a seat in the rocking chair and watched as Ruby hovered over Page. They seemed to be good for each other, a fact that warmed his heart. "Are you sure you're up for this? I can come back another time."

Ruby eyed him as Page shook her head. "I'll be fine. Just tell us what you found out about Ruby's father."

Ruby slid down to take a seat on the floor next to the sofa. "Did you find my dad?"

He shook his head and flipped to the page in his legal pad where he'd written his notes. "I don't have one Thomas Burns that it could be. I have two."

Page frowned. "Two possibilities?"

"They both fit the time line that we know

about Ruby's mother. They were in Oklahoma at the same time. Both originally from Detroit. And both are about the age that your mother would be."

Ruby didn't say anything, but stared at him. He wasn't sure if this was welcome news or not. Her expression remained like stone, not giving away anything about what she was thinking. Page, however, seemed to take the news harder. "So what do we do next?"

"I'll contact both men to see if they knew a Marcia Wilson, your mom, and we'll go from there." He set the legal pad on the coffee table. "And there's something else we need to talk about."

He could see both of them tense up.

"I received copies of your birth certificate, Ruby, as well as your mother's death certificate. It listed a relative."

"Yeah. Me."

He shook his head. "Your grandmother, Sheilah."

Page looked at Ruby and then at him. "What does that mean? That she gets custody of Ruby now?"

Mateo sat forward in his chair. "Did your

mother ever mention Sheilah? Do you remember meeting her?"

"Mama said that it was just us in this world. That we only had each other. I don't know who Sheilah is."

"To be honest, I'm not quite willing to see you go to someone who we don't know. Who may not be a fit parent. After all, your mom had severed all ties with her for some reason." Mateo glanced at Page. "We need more information before we pursue that path. Is that okay with the both of you?"

Ruby nodded vigorously as Page watched her. "I think we should proceed with caution. Not only with Thomas Burns, but with Sheilah as well. Ruby is the one we need to be thinking about first."

"I agree."

He sat watching Page, her color so pale. "Do you need anything?"

"Nope. Ruby's been taking good care of me."

At the mention of her name, the girl stood. "I'm going to take the food in the kitchen and eat, so you two can talk."

After she left, Page smirked at Mateo. "I

think that was her subtle way of giving us some privacy."

"It worked." He settled farther into the rocking chair. "How are you really feeling?"

"Mateo, I know about your history with your mom, so you don't have to do this."

"We're friends, right? And friends help each other out. What can I do?"

She sighed and closed her eyes, lying back on the pillow. "Nothing. I just need to rest."

"I can make sure meals are brought over."

"April is taking care of that."

"I can drive you to your doctor's appointments."

"Again, April."

"There must be something I can do."

"You can go home." She opened her eyes. "I don't want you to see me like this, Mateo. I don't want this to be your image of me."

He knew what she meant. Otherwise, he might focus on the cancer, and not her. He took the legal pad from the coffee table and stood. "I'll go so you can sleep. I'll keep up with my search and give you both an update when I've found out anything more."

Page started to sit up, but he waved her back down. "You don't need to see me out. I'll talk to you later."

"Thanks for letting us know where we stand."

"Take care of yourself."

He walked to the door, followed by Ruby. He turned to the girl. "If she needs anything, can you let me know? She has my number."

Ruby nodded and opened the front door for him. "Are you gonna really find my dad?"

"I think we've got a great start." He put a hand on her shoulder. "Don't give up, kiddo."

She tried to smile, but it didn't quite reach her eyes. Instead, she seemed more worried about finding her father than she had before. He tried not to read too much into that. He hoped he was doing the right thing, not just for Ruby, but for Page, too.

CHAPTER SEVEN

THE ROOM WOULDN'T stop spinning. Page hung on to the dresser as she tried to make it across the bedroom to the bathroom. It looked so far away, and a wave of heat swept over her. It was still dark out, and the bedside digital clock read that it wasn't quite dawn. She took a step, but the floor shifted and she stumbled closer to the bed.

Something was wrong.

Rivulets of sweat seemed to be starting behind her ears and flowing down her neck. She'd had hot flashes in the past due to the treatment of her breast cancer, but this was not one of those. This was something else.

Slowly, she made it to the door to her bedroom. She gripped the door frame and tried to peek across the hall into Ruby's room. "Ruby," she called out, but she couldn't speak much above a whisper.

She fell to her knees, feeling as if something was pushing her to the floor. She called Ruby's name again, then closed her eyes, unable to keep them open any longer.

When she woke, she found a familiar paramedic taking her vitals. She blinked at him and tried to turn her head to where Ruby stood watching them, her hand covering her mouth. "I'm okay."

The paramedic frowned at her and pointed to his partner, who was carrying a stretcher. "You have a temperature approaching one-oh-five. You're anything but okay. Miss, we're going to take Page to the hospital. Are you coming with us?"

Ruby nodded, but Page tried to sit up. "I don't need to go to the hospital, Gary."

"You're a nurse. If one of your patients had collapsed with a dangerously high temperature, what would you recommend?"

She sighed and closed her eyes. "Fine. But I can walk." She tried to move, but lacked the energy and fell back to the floor.

"Not on my watch."

Gary and his partner carried her to the ambulance. Ruby followed behind them and got in the back of the vehicle with Page. The girl looked ashen, as if she might pass out, too. Page held out her hand and Ruby moved forward to grasp it. “I was so scared when I found you in the hallway. I didn’t know what to do, so I called 911.”

“You did the right thing.” Page closed her eyes and willed away the waves of nausea that threatened. “Do you have my phone still?” Ruby nodded. “Good. When we get to the hospital, call April.”

“I already did that. When I was waiting for the ambulance to arrive. She said she’d meet us at the emergency room.”

Page closed her eyes, unable to keep them open a moment longer. She felt so tired. Tired and scared. She knew there was something wrong, different than what she’d experienced before. And knowing that she was making Ruby go through it with her made her feel even more terrified about what was happening. “I’m sorry I scared you.”

“It’s not your fault.”

Page gave a wry grin. “I guess we’ll blame the cancer.” She lost the grin and squeezed Ruby’s hand. “I’m glad you were there. If you hadn’t, I don’t know how long I might have been there.”

Ruby nodded and wiped away her tears with her free hand. “Me, too.”

The ambulance arrived at Detroit General and Ruby sat back as they moved the stretcher with Page. The placed it on a gurney and wheeled her into the ER. They were met by Kenny, the overnight ER doctor, as well as April. Page knew she was in good hands, so she closed her eyes once again.

Voices floated around her as well as bright lights. She could feel her body being moved from the gurney to a hospital bed. A prick in her arm told her that an IV had been inserted. Cool cloths on her head, chest, arms and legs. More voices.

She wanted to tell them that she was fine. She was a little warm, but she didn’t need such attention. She felt as if she was lying in a warm bath, her ears underwater so that sounds were distorted and muffled. Her body felt heavy, her limbs unable to lift or move.

The need to sleep grew until it became the only thing she wanted in the whole world. She tuned out what was going on around her and accepted oblivion.

MATEO HADN'T ARRIVED at the office yet, but his cell phone was buzzing. He pulled over and glanced at the caller ID. Sherri's name popped up. "Hey, cuz."

"Where are you?"

An odd question on a Friday morning. "On my way to work. Where are you?"

"At Detroit General."

Okay, that wasn't the answer he'd been expecting. "Are you all right?"

"I'm fine. It's Page."

His heart stopped for a few seconds. "What's—"

"She's really sick, Mateo."

He froze. Wasn't sure what to say. Didn't know what to do. He had just seen her, and she'd been fine. Nauseous and tired, but not needing a hospital.

"Mateo?"

"I'm still here." He gripped the phone tighter. "What do you want me to do?"

His cousin sighed loudly and said some things in Spanish that would have made their parents blush. "Know what? Don't do anything. But I thought you actually cared for her."

He did, maybe too much. "Sherri, I don't

know what you expect from me. She was okay yesterday. What happened?"

"Complications from an infection. You know how the treatment affects the immune system."

He certainly did. "Thank you for letting me know."

"I'm more than calling to just tell you. You need to come up here."

"What can I do besides sit in a waiting room?"

"If she's in the hospital, how does that affect her foster-care situation? You can be so dense sometimes."

He started to protest, but realized that she'd hung up already. He pulled his car back onto the road and eased into traffic. He spotted his office up ahead, but passed it. It wouldn't hurt for him to check in on Page and see if Ruby had somewhere to go if they admitted Page. Sherri had been right. He needed to be the lawyer, at least.

He arrived at the hospital, parked and went inside. "I'm here for Page Kosinski," he said to the receptionist.

"They took her upstairs. Check in with the intake nurse for her room number." She looked past him to someone standing behind him.

Mateo stepped back into her line of vision. “Is she okay?”

“I can’t give you that information since you’re not family. Now step aside.”

He apologized to the person waiting behind him and left the emergency room. He entered the atrium, where windows and tall ceilings spilled light into the corridor. A desk manned by two women had a line of about four people. When he reached the front, he asked for Page’s room number. One of them typed her name into the computer then frowned at the screen. “She’s on the sixth floor in ICU.” She pointed to the elevators behind her. “Go up to six, turn left and follow the red arrows. The nurse at the ward desk will direct you further.”

He nodded. Getting an elevator to take him up the sixth floor seemed to take forever.

By the time the elevator reached the sixth floor, his patience had evaporated. He found the red arrows painted on the walls to the left and followed them. He spotted Sherri. He walked up to her and hugged her, not knowing what else to do. She hugged him back and then smacked him upside the head. "About time you got here."

"I drove here as soon as I hung up with you."

Sherri narrowed her eyes at him. "Okay."

She stepped back, and he saw that April and Ruby sat in chairs behind her. He rushed forward and took turns hugging them both. "Have you heard anything?"

"The infection is attacking her organs, and her immune system is too weak to fight it," April said. "Thank goodness Ruby was there to find her and call for an ambulance."

Mateo noticed the girl looked shaken. "But the ICU?"

"Any infection with cancer elevates the risk, so they're not playing around. Right now, they're trying to bring her body temp down and determine the cause to treat it." April winced. "If the infection is viral, it could get tricky."

Mateo remembered the infection that his mother had fought and lost to. It was in the ICU that she had finally let go of her family and her life. He tried to shake the memory, but was failing. "How long do they think she'll be here?"

"A few days, maybe a week. Depends on how well she responds to treatment."

"I know it's probably not what we want to talk about right now, but what about Ruby?"

April glanced at the girl. "She can stay with me until Page is better."

Sherri shook her head. "You're about to get married. You don't have time. Dez and I have space for her."

Mateo agreed. "Sherri makes a good point."

April crossed her arms over her chest. "I'm not getting married if Page can't be there, so that's a moot point. Ruby's staying with me."

"What about what I want?"

They turned to look at the girl. Mateo gestured to her. "Right. What do you want to do, Ruby?"

The girl bit her lip. "I want to stay here with Page. I can sleep in the waiting room and eat in the cafeteria."

April went over to Ruby and put an arm around her shoulder. "Sweetie, I know you care about Page, but you also have to think about your baby. Would that be what's best for all of you?"

"I want to be close if she needs me."

Mateo considered her words, amazed at how much the girl had grown to care for Page in such a short time. "I'm with April. Any one of us would be willing to bring you up here to stay with Page during the day, but you should go home at night with someone, either April or Sherri." He glanced at his cousin, who nodded.

April said, "Mateo's right. Page wouldn't want anything to happen to you, Ruby, or the baby. And maybe the best place right now is with Sherri."

Ruby looked as if she wanted to argue, but then nodded. "Fine." She removed herself from April's grip and went to sit in a chair.

Mateo glanced at Sherri. "Since you're already approved to be a foster parent, I'll file a temporary change of custody of Ruby to you."

April grimaced. "This is going to hurt Page and her chances of adopting Ruby's baby, isn't it?"

“It certainly won’t help, but I’ll worry about that later. Right now, my priority is Ruby.” He put a hand on Sherri’s shoulder. “I’ll get the paperwork to you as soon as I can.” He glanced at the ward nurse, who was guarding the ICU entrance. “Is there any way I can get in to see Page?”

April gave a soft nod. “I’ll see what I can do. But she might not be awake.” She left the waiting room.

Sherri nudged him. “I’m glad you decided to come.”

“You know how hard it is for me to be back here.” The memories threatened to choke him. “But you were right. I’m her lawyer, and she needs me to act on her behalf right now.”

“You’re a lot more than just her lawyer, so when are you going to admit it?”

April returned to them. “I can take you back to see her, Mateo, but you can only stay for ten minutes.”

Ruby popped up. “Can I come?”

April looked between them. “Okay.”

April ushered Mateo and Ruby to the ward nurse, who pressed a button. With a loud buzzing, the doors to the wing swung open. Ruby took Mateo's hand as the nurse guided them back to Page's room.

Page was lying on a bed hooked up with wires and tubes connected to machines that beeped and clicked. Her body was covered by silver blankets. "They're cooling blankets to lower her temperature," the nurse told them.

Ruby asked, "Is she awake?"

"She might be. Go ahead and talk to her."

Ruby stepped forward, but didn't let go of Mateo's hand. She placed her other hand on the top of Page's bald head. "You have to get better. April threatened to take me shopping for a dress for her wedding, and you know how I feel about that." The girl tried to smile, but the corners of her mouth turned down. "Please don't die, too."

Mateo heard the girl's plea and felt his heart break. How he'd once asked the same of his mom.

The girl started to cry and turned into Mateo's arms. He comforted her, keeping his gaze on Page, reminding himself that it wasn't his mother he saw lying in the bed. Instead, she had a flush in her cheeks that spoke of vitality. Not the pallor that he had expected.

He rubbed Ruby's back. "She's not going to die. She has a lot to live for."

They all did.

MATEO HAD JUST finished filing the temporary change in foster placement for Ruby at the county courthouse, when someone called his name. He spotted Greg Novakowski, his friend Jack's father, and another Detroit cop coming toward him. He waited for the older man to reach him then held out his hand. "Good to see you, Greg."

"Meeting a client?"

"Dropping off paperwork. You here on a case?"

"Had lunch with your buddy, Judge Gorges. Do you have a moment to talk over a cup of coffee?"

Mateo glanced at his watch. He'd been hoping to stop by the hospital to check on Page. But Greg wouldn't have stopped him if it hadn't been important. "Sure. Lolly's, around the corner?"

At the diner, Greg held up two fingers to the waitress who greeted them. They were seated in a booth by the window. Mateo glanced outside and wondered what this could be about. He knew Greg by reputation and through Jack, of course. He'd been a cop for more years than Mateo had been alive. Rumor had it that he was looking to retire. They ordered coffee and Mateo waited to hear what the older man had to say.

Once the waitress placed two mugs of coffee in front of them, Greg added cream to his and stirred slowly. "You know that Judge Gorges and I have been friends since my rookie days?"

"No, sir, I wasn't aware."

"He's concerned about you."

"No reason he should be."

The older man eyed him, and Mateo had the urge to squirm in his seat. "He's said he hasn't seen you in his courtroom for a while."

"Isn't that a good thing?"

"Only if that meant your neighborhood crime rates were down." He took a sip. "So are they?"

Mateo was aware that Greg knew very well that they weren't. Especially since he lived only a few streets from where Mateo had grown up. "I'm not taking juvenile-crime cases any more. I'm focusing on family law. Divorce. Adoptions. Child-custody cases."

"Uh-huh."

What was he supposed to say? He felt like he was being reprimanded by his father rather than by a friend. "I can't take juvie cases any longer." The man must have been an excellent interrogator. He had the cold stare down pat and obviously knew how to use silence to motivate the suspect to speak. In this case, Mateo felt as guilty as sin. "What do you want me to say?"

"Let me tell you how I see it. You're burnt out. I get it. We all get that way from time to time. But the key is not to stay out of the game, but to get refreshed and go back in." Greg leaned forward. "Did Jack ever tell you that I took a six-month leave from the force?"

Mateo mentally reviewed the stories that Jack had told him over the years. "No, sir."

"Like you, I got sick of the gang violence. Young guys trapped in the unending cycle of poverty and crime. It never goes away entirely, though sometimes things do get better."

"Except my clients keep getting younger."

"Maybe. The point is, I didn't give up. I went back to the force, determined to make a difference. And I hope that after all these years, I have."

"I haven't given up. Not entirely." Greg peered at him until Mateo sighed. "Okay. I gave up. But my heart couldn't take watching most of these kids enter the prison system and come out hardened criminals. It never ends."

"I don't know what you want from me—"

"I want you to get your fire back. What happened to that young lawyer out to save the world? What happened to the guy who helped connect troubled youth to upstanding men and women to show them a better way?"

"I told you. He got tired of seeing his efforts result in nothing."

"Nothing? You're responsible for many young folks having graduated high school and gone on to college or the military. One young woman got into Harvard on a full-ride scholarship because of the meeting you set up between her and my daughter, Shelby."

"And for each one of them, I have six who are sitting in jail or buried in the cemetery."

"So we give up on the ones we might be able to help?"

Mateo stood and pulled out a few bills from his wallet and threw them on the table. "Greg, I appreciate your concern, but there's nothing you can say to change my mind."

"Don't give up on the neighborhood that didn't give up on you."

Mateo didn't look back as he exited the diner. Determined to visit Detroit General, he hustled back to his car. Greg didn't know what he was talking about, he told himself. He hadn't lost his fire. Wasn't he helping Page with not just the foster care of Ruby, but now the adoption of her baby? He might not be taking juvenile crime cases, but he could still help his neighborhood by doing these things.

By the time he arrived at the hospital, he'd almost convinced himself that he was still making the same difference. He thought of Scotty sitting in the adult jail and shook off his doubts.

He strode into the hospital and took the elevator to the sixth floor. The route had become too familiar. Page had been in ICU for the entire weekend. While her doctor was optimistic that she was fighting the infection, her pale and silent form seemed to contradict his words.

Mateo stopped in the waiting room and noticed that none of her friends were present. He could have checked the cafeteria, or perhaps they were visiting Page's room.

"Mateo, you're here." Ruby rushed in and greeted him. Ruby put her arms around his waist, resting her head on his chest. "She looks better today."

April, who had followed Ruby, gave a small nod. "She has a little more color."

"That's good news." He patted Ruby on the shoulder, and she released him. "Do you think they'll let me see her?"

"Probably in a half hour or so. The nurses are in the middle of a shift change and going over the notes on each patient." April pawed through her purse and handed Ruby a few dollar bills. "Can you do me a favor and get me a bottled water from the cafeteria?"

The girl nodded and left the waiting room.

April sat in a chair and motioned for Mateo to sit next to her and he did so. "I didn't want to say this in front of her, but the infection seems to be spreading despite the medical team's efforts."

"What does that mean?" he asked.

April rested her elbows on her knees. "It means she's still got a huge fight ahead of her. I can't believe I'm admitting this but I'm kind of starting to lose hope."

"Hey." Mateo nudged her arm and April looked up at him with wet eyes. "Page is a fighter."

"I know. But sometimes the battle is too big. I know I'm supposed to be the optimistic one. That I should be saying we need to stay positive, and not to give up. But I'm afraid of losing my best friend."

Mateo put his arm around her shoulders and pulled her against his side. "I'm scared of that, too."

"Page is the one who always hopes for the best, but expects the worst." April took a deep breath and squared her shoulders. "No. I'm not going to give in to my fears. I'm going to expect her to recover. I'm planning on her standing beside me at my wedding next week." She gave a sharp nod at her words. "She will recover."

He wasn't sure what to say. Wanting to agree, he was still worried for Page.

"She's going to be waking up soon and making us look like fools for doubting her."

He blinked, wishing he had such faith and hope.

When his turn came to visit Page, he walked into the room alone. Sat in the chair beside her bed and took her hand in his. Her color looked worse than it had before. How could this be the same woman he'd walked with by the Detroit River not too long ago?

He pressed her hand to his cheek and closed his eyes. "Please fight this, Page. We all need you."

He opened his eyes and peered at her. No response. "*I* need you, so you have to get better. Come back to me."

A machine started to blare, and Mateo looked around to see what was wrong. A group of nurses ran in and immediately began pressing buttons on the machine. One checked her heart rate while another prepared a syringe. One of them looked at Mateo. “I’m sorry, sir. We have to ask you to step out.”

“Is she okay?”

“Please, sir.”

Mateo backed out of the room as a doctor pushed past him and started shouting orders to the nursing staff. He stood for several minutes watching them work on Page.

The more he watched, the more scared he felt, so he ambled back to the waiting room. April glanced up at him as he entered. “You’re all white. What happened?”

“I don’t know. A machine started going off, and a bunch of staff rushed in. They asked me to leave.”

April brought up a hand to her mouth and closed her eyes. “Please, Page. Fight this.”

Mateo sank into the closest chair. He had hoped to guard his heart from exactly this kind of worry. And yet, here he sat in the hospital, waiting for word on her condition. It wasn’t supposed to have happened. She was supposed to be a client only, maybe even a friend. But this ache in his chest spoke of more than friendship.

After an excruciating wait, a doctor entered the waiting room and approached April. Mateo stood and joined them. “She stopped breathing for a moment, but we were able to clear her airways. She’s resting peaceably now.”

April nodded. “Thank you, Brad. We appreciate the update.”

“So she’s not dying?” Mateo croaked.

“No. She’s still fighting.” The doctor gave him a soft smile. “Her refusal to give up just might save her.”

“I hope so.”

The doctor left the room, and April sat down again. Mateo took the chair next to her. “I thought we’d lost her…” he said.

“I know.” She used her thumb to wipe away the moisture from her eyes. “We can’t give up on her, though.” She peered at him. “Have you?”

Mateo wasn’t sure how to answer that. He held on to the hope that she’d recover, but he wasn’t sure if he could wish for anything more.

PAGE OPENED HER EYES and glanced around the room. Okay, she wasn't at home. The beige painted walls and medical equipment told her that she was in the hospital. She tried to sit up, but it took too much effort so she eased back down. A call button had been tied to the metal barrier on the side of her bed, so she pushed it. What seemed like an hour later, but surely wasn't, a nurse entered the room. "You're awake." The nurse started to take her vitals.

"How long have I been asleep?"

The nurse made notes on her tablet. "Almost seventy-two hours. There's family waiting to see you and I'll call the doctor to let him know you're awake."

Family? Please don't let her mother be here. She could handle almost anything except that. Her mouth was dry, but it didn't seem like she had any water. She'd probably have to ask for ice chips when the nurse returned.

The door to her room opened and April and Ruby burst inside. Page sighed with relief. Ruby ran toward her and put her arms around her, crying. "I thought you were never going to wake up."

Page looked over Ruby's shoulder to April. "What happened?"

"You came down with a bacterial infection that raised your temperature. They've been pumping you full of antibiotics to fight it." April sat on the edge of the hospital bed. "But I agree with Ruby. It seemed you were never going to wake up."

Ruby took a step back and wiped her face. "How are you feeling?"

"Tired." Page closed her eyes for a moment. "Like all I want to do is sleep."

April said, "We won't stay long, but I wanted to make sure that you were okay."

Page opened her eyes. "I'm fine, but tired."

Dr. Brad Wittman, a friend and colleague, came into the room. "I'll be the judge of that." He glanced at April and Ruby, who took turns touching Page's hand before leaving with promises to visit later.

Page adjusted the blankets around her. "Okay, Brad. Give it to me straight."

He put the stethoscope in his ears and listened to her breathing sounds and heartbeat for a moment then nodded and stepped back. "Good news is that you're on the upswing. A few more days of antibiotics and rest, and you'll be fine."

"And the bad news?"

"You'll probably feel as if you've been run over by a truck for a while. Because of the cancer, it's going to take you longer to bounce back." He peered into her face as if to gauge her reaction. "That means being off work for at least the next two to three weeks. I'd say to be on bed rest, but I know better than trying to keep you down for that long."

"You've got to be joking. Two to three weeks?"

He looked her over. "I'll make you a deal. If you can get out of that bed and walk across the room, I'll change it to a week of bed rest."

Fine. She'd prove that she could do this. She struggled to get the blankets off, but the effort overwhelmed her. Finally, she laid back on the pillows. "You win."

"Figured I'd might. I'll get you moved to a step-down unit now that you're awake. We'll get you up and moving tomorrow. As soon as you can make a lap around the ward, I'll send you home. But I'm serious,

Page. No working. Only resting. Or you could end up back here."

She frowned at him. "Trust me. That's the last thing I want."

"I'll get your transfer started. In the meantime, I'll send your friends back to see you. They've been living in the waiting room since you were brought in."

Brad left and moments later the door to her room opened. Sherri entered first, followed by a pale-looking Mateo. "You gave us such a scare," Sherri said.

"Sorry about that."

Sherri hugged her and then let go. Page looked up at Mateo. He stayed several feet away from her, his back to the wall, and then he began speaking. "I've placed Ruby in Sherri's care until you're 100 percent better. Judge Bond signed off on it and expects to be kept updated on your condition. He also asked for a progress report on the search for Ruby's family."

Page frowned at the cold, professional tone he used. He could barely look at her, wouldn't approach her. What was his problem?

PAGE SEEMED SO FRAGILE. So unlike the feisty woman that he knew. He kept the conversation on a professional level because he couldn't trust himself to make it more personal. If he did, he might end up crying and clinging to her.

He thought he'd lost her last night. When he'd been given permission to visit her and he'd sat at her bedside, holding her hand. Willing her to wake up. And then machines had started blaring, and medical personnel had pushed him out of the way. He'd hoped, prayed, that she'd be okay. But at the same time, he knew that he couldn't pursue anything with her. That he wouldn't sign up for a future of hospital rooms only to end their relationship at a grave site.

Finally, he shifted his eyes so he was looking right at her, and she frowned at him. "What did Judge Bond say about my adoption petition?"

Did she really want more bad news? He cleared his throat. "He recommended that the proceedings be placed on hold until Ruby gives birth and your health improves." *If it improves* had been the judge's actual words.

"Right." The sour expression on Page's face told him exactly what she was thinking. "I'm fighting a lost cause, aren't I?" She sighed and her shoulders sagged. "Ruby will be so disappointed."

Sherri put a hand on her shoulder. "What about you?"

Page looked up at her. "Not sure I actually expected it to happen. Hoped it would, but I figured something like that wouldn't be possible for me. I'm sorry that I wasted your time, Mateo."

He couldn't stand to see her looking so defeated. "Don't throw in the towel just yet. You're a lot better than when I saw you last night."

Her eyes widened at his admission. "You were here?"

Sherri nodded. "He's been here every night since they've admitted you. Claims that he's watching out for his client, but… whatever."

Mateo wanted the floor to swallow him up. Page was paying him to look out for her interests, he'd told himself numerous times. And he'd done just that with getting Ruby into temporary foster care with his cousin and keeping Page's hopes of adoption alive. He'd found a British case where a single woman fighting cancer had successfully adopted a toddler. When he'd brought it to the judge's attention, Bond had warned him that one foreign scenario wouldn't hold much sway. Especially considering Page's current situation.

Mateo so admired that Page's first thought had been for Ruby and her feelings. She seemed to always put other people's feelings ahead of her own. He admired that. More than that, he loved the woman.

If only...

He looked around the room. "I should get going. Let Ruby come back again to see you."

"Will you return later?"

He tried to ignore the hope in Page's voice. His cousin stared, waiting for his answer. He gave a short nod. "Yes. Sure. Glad to see you doing better."

He left the room quickly and returned to the waiting area. "Ruby, you can go back and see her."

The girl smiled and almost ran down the

hall at his words. April asked, "Did you tell her the news?"

"I told her that the adoption is on hold. That Ruby is staying with Sherri."

April eyed him. "What about Ruby's father?"

"That can wait until she's stronger. I haven't even told Ruby that I found him."

"You can't keep it to yourself much longer."

"I shouldn't have told Sherri, but she overheard the conversation and made conclusions on her own."

"Page is stronger than you give her credit for. She can handle whatever is thrown at her."

"I'm realizing that now."

He greeted Dez and Zach before taking off. Page's friends had rallied around her, which was good to see. Hopefully they'd do the same when Ruby met her dad.

"YOU ARE NOT postponing the wedding." Page stared at April. Her condition had been improving and she hoped to be released by the end of the week, so there was no way she'd allow her best friend to do anything as crazy as change her wedding date. Plans had been made. Dresses bought. A hall reserved and food ordered. “You can’t do it.”

“I won’t get married without you.” April set down the magazine she’d been reading. “So it can wait.”

“What does Zach say?”

April smiled at the mention of his name. “That he’ll go along with whatever I want.”

“That’s sweet of you to offer to wait for me, but I can’t let you throw away everything you’ve been working toward.”

“If you’re not out by this weekend, then we’ll wait.”

Brad walked into the hospital room. “Did I hear someone is ready to go home?”

April stood and moved so that he could get closer to Page. “Yes, doctor. I’m supposed to get married this weekend with Page as my maid of honor. But I told her that we can wait.”

“And I told April that she can’t postpone,” Page insisted.

The doctor removed his stethoscope from his ears and smiled. “What if April didn’t have to?”

Page frowned. "What? Like getting married here at the hospital?"

"No, what you said. About going home. The nurses told me you've been making circles around the floor. Your temp is down. Your energy is slowly coming up. I'd say we can send you home today."

When Page stared at him with an open mouth, he said, "Unless, of course, you'd rather stay."

"If you're kidding, Brad—"

"But I want you to rest when you get home and no working for at least two weeks. Nothing more strenuous than walking and no dancing, unless it's slow." Brad put a hand on April's shoulder. "Congratulations, by the way."

"Thanks!" April clapped her hands. "This is the best news ever."

Page shrugged. "Some hot Hollywood actor coming as my date would be the best news ever, but I'll take this." She started to scoot toward the edge of the bed so that she could change into her clothes. "I'm hoping that you'll drive me home."

April handed her the plastic bag with her belongings. "Of course, I will. And I'll stay with you and Ruby until the wedding. My house is packed and ready to be moved over to Zach's anyway."

"I don't need a babysitter."

"Funny. Your foster daughter said the same thing." April pulled the curtain around the hospital bed to give Page some privacy.

It's funny, but the word *daughter* made Page smile. She'd missed living with Ruby. Seeing her face every day. She missed their routine together. Talking at night while the TV droned in the background. Eating breakfast together in the morning. Even the tiny things like seeing Ruby's toothbrush in the cup next to hers gave her a sense of completeness.

"I'll be glad to be home."

"You'll need to be careful, though. This infection was a bad one." April sobered and sat on the bed next to Page and put her arm around her. "I don't know what I'd do without my best friend."

"I'm hoping you don't have to find out for a long time."

They sat together for a moment, then April sighed and stood. "I'm going to order the wheelchair now because I know how long it can take for them to send one up. Do you need anything else?"

"Just Ruby and my discharge papers."

April exited and Page got dressed, then finally slumped on the edge of the bed. Putting her clothes on had worn her out, and she still had to get home. She figured she'd probably take a nap once she was settled.

Ruby popped her head into the room and smiled at her. "April said you're coming home."

Page held her arms out to the girl, and she walked quickly over and hugged her. "Which means you're coming home, too, right?"

"I've missed you."

"You won't believe how much I missed you." Page put the back of her hand on the girl's forehead. "How are you feeling?"

Ruby took a step back. "Good. No pains at all. But the baby sure is moving."

"I bet." Page put a hand on her rounded belly. "Maybe we can ask April to take us both to your next appointment." She paused. "Wait. She'll be on her honeymoon. Maybe Sherri will take us."

"What did the doctor say about you?"

"I'll need to take it easy for a few weeks. He won't let me go back to work right away."

"More time with me, I guess." Ruby grinned and nudged her shoulder.

"So what have I missed?"

"I went to another meeting with the other teen moms."

"How did that go?"

Ruby shrugged. "One of the girls, Lauren, had her baby this past week. She was downstairs in the maternity ward, so I went to visit her."

Page was touched by Ruby's kindness. "How'd that go?"

"Kind of emotional." Ruby looked away. "She decided to give the baby up, she was so sad."

"It's got to be hard to let go in a situation like that."

"Will it be like that for me?" Ruby asked. "I mean, Lauren knew she was doing the right thing for the baby, but it still made her cry. I'm not sure anything I said to her helped."

"You were sweet to try, though."

Ruby stretched. "Can we talk about something else?"

"School starts next week. I wonder if we should get you registered."

Ruby shook her head vigorously. "Can't you homeschool me or something? I know I brought up that alternative school, but you need me around to make sure you're okay."

Page considered it. She didn't know the first thing about teaching. She probably needed to register something with the state. Maybe Mateo would be able to help her through the process.

April entered and smiled at them both. "The nurse is going to come and unhook your IV, and the wheelchair is on its way. Are you ready to go home?"

Page grinned and nodded. "More than ready."

PAGE LEFT ANOTHER message on Mateo's phone. After she hung up, her cell phone started to buzz. She answered it, hoping it was him. "Mateo?"

"It's your mother."

She wanted to groan, but kept it to herself. "I was hoping it was my lawyer."

"What in the world do you need a lawyer for?"

Page weighed how much to share with her mother. "I'm in the middle of adopting."

"Oh, Page." Disappointment dripped through in her voice. "Why in the world would you put yourself through that?"

"Maybe because I always wanted to be a mother."

"Trust me. It's not all it's cracked up to be."

Page bit back a comment about her lack of mothering skills being a huge factor in that and concentrated instead on the positives. Ruby had a good home with her. And soon, so might Ruby's baby. "What do you want, Mother?"

"Can't I call just to chat?"

That wasn't like her. "I don't have time to talk right now. So just say what you want to and get it over with."

Her mother cleared her throat. "I have an eye-doctor appointment next Wednesday and they're putting those drops in my eyes so I won't be able to drive. You need to pick me up at two."

"No."

"Why not? Because of the cancer?"

"I just got out of the hospital. I almost died."

There was pause on the other end. Page waited, wondering what words of discouragement her mother would offer. Her mother huffed. "Fine. Be selfish. I'll make other arrangements. Goodbye."

Page stared at the phone, checking to make sure she actually had hung up. Conversations with her mother usually drained her, and this one had been no different. She couldn't understand why the woman couldn't be happy for her just once. Couldn't say something like "Good luck, Page. You're a strong woman, and I know it will work out for you. You're going to be fine." Was it any wonder that Page doubted herself when her own mother didn't believe in her?

Ruby brought two large glasses of iced tea from the kitchen and handed one to Page. "Who was on the phone?"

"My mother."

Ruby made a face. "Oh. Sorry."

Page laughed.

"April told me more about her. We had

a lot of time to talk in the waiting room this past week." Ruby took a sip of her tea and made a face. "I added too much sugar. Sure can't make sweet tea like my mama could."

Page tasted her own tea, and her lips puckered. "I guess there's a learning curve."

Ruby stood and tried to take her glass away. "I'll fix it."

She kept a hold of the glass. "It's fine. Don't worry." She patted the sofa next to her. "Take a seat. We need to talk about something."

"Uh-oh. I know that look." But Ruby sat down.

Page put her glass on the coffee table and held out her hand. When the girl put her hand in hers, she tried to think of how to say what she needed to say. "Mateo talked to me. Because of my health, the judge is concerned that I won't be able to provide the right home for your baby."

Ruby's bottom lip protruded. "So you're not going to adopt it? I thought you wanted it."

"I do." Emotion clogged her throat, and she coughed to clear it. "I do, but Mateo wanted to warn me that the adoption won't be an easy process. We've got to prove that I'm well enough to care for an infant."

"Oh." Ruby let go of her hand. "But what if it's what I want? Don't I get a say in this?"

"You will, and that will help our case. But I want you to be aware of what might happen."

"Can't you look on the bright side of things? Maybe you're worried about nothing. Maybe you need this baby as much as it needs you." Ruby stood. "I need you to believe, Page. Because I'm scared enough on my own."

The girl left the room, and Page tried to get to her feet, but lacked the energy. She called Ruby's name, but she didn't respond.

She wished she could believe, but her history had proven that good things didn't come to her. Instead, she got handed more pain, more disease, more loss. Maybe she was Nurse Doom and Gloom, who had a storm cloud following her. Could she be positive for once? Could she believe like Ruby wanted her to?

For Ruby, she would try.

THE CLOUDY SKY threatened rain as Mateo stepped out of his car at the cemetery. He'd been thinking of his mother quite a bit that week. He scooped up the bouquet of flowers he'd purchased and locked the car. The walk to his mother's grave site took only a moment.

He stared down at the marker. *Lucia Maria Estevez Lopez. Beloved wife and mother.* He bent down and removed the leaves and weeds that covered the stone and placed the daisies, her favorite flower, beside it. "Hi, Mom. Miss you."

He placed his hand on the stone marker. "I'm sorry I haven't been here more often, but being here only makes me feel the loss of you even more."

Was he crazy for talking to this stone? For thinking that he could somehow find answers to his troubles by being here? He adjusted the flowers on the grave and patted it before standing and looking down. She'd been so young, only ten years older than he was now. How could her life have been cut so short? It wasn't fair. She hadn't deserved it. She should be alive to see Lulu getting married and now, expecting a baby.

She'd missed out, and he wanted to kick the stone to prove how unjust it all was.

"I've met someone, Mom. I wish you could know her because I think you'd like her." He thought of Page's recent stay at the hospital. "I want something to happen with her, but I'm scared. Afraid of losing her like I lost you."

He rubbed his left eye, which burned. This is why he didn't come out here. It only made him feel worse. He put his hand again on the gravestone. "Goodbye, Mom."

He walked back to his car and sat inside, promising himself that he wouldn't face any more situations that made him feel so lonely and angry. He would fill his life with only good things. Yet he couldn't avoid pain no matter what he did. Was that the point of life? To be in pain? It didn't make sense. But then there wasn't much in his life right now that did make sense.

Maybe you were supposed to find a way to go on through the pain. To find the joy in spite of the tears.

He started the car and drove away.

CHAPTER EIGHT

THE IMAGE IN the mirror stared back at Page as she rubbed a hand over her bald head. She could ignore the dark circles under her eyes. In fact, she had makeup that would cover those up. But the glare off the top of her head was hard to pretend wasn't there.

She'd been bald for most of the last three years. Seemed as soon as she'd finished one round of chemotherapy, she'd grow back stubble then suffer a reoccurrence of cancer and be back to being without hair. She tried to remember the last time she'd been able to run her fingers through it and couldn't recall.

In her closet on the top shelf, Page had a box, the contents of which might help her out. She used a hanger to reach the box and nudged it toward the edge of the shelf so she could reach it on tiptoe. She placed the box on her bed, opened the lid and stared down into it.

She took out the dark brown wig and fluffed the hair. In a rare moment of nurturing, her mother had bought it for her during her first round of chemo. Page put it on her head now and walked to the mirror. She checked how the wig looked and adjusted it so that the part was in the middle, the length of hair reaching her shoulders. Pulling the strands this way and that, she debated about wearing it. She looked almost normal. Almost healthy. But the image of herself in the mirror didn't match how she felt inside, or who she really was. Still…

The front door opened, and Page heard Ruby greet April. She nodded and walked down the hall to the living room. April stared at Page while Ruby smothered a snicker. "What in the world are you wearing?" April asked.

Page stopped abruptly and looked down at the soft gray dress she wore. They'd agreed on this one. "Oh, this." She reached up to touch the wig. Had it slipped? No, it felt like it was in place. "Is it on wrong?"

"The problem is that it's on at all." April frowned. "Why are you wearing it?"

"You don't want a maid of honor with a bald head in your pictures."

"I do if it's you. This—" April plucked the wig off her head "—is not you."

Page sighed. "April, these are pictures that you and Zach are going to be looking at for the rest of your lives. Think about it." She snatched back the hair. "I'm wearing it."

"Is it comfortable? Do you feel better about yourself in it?" April rhymed off the questions. Why was she interrogating her? How did she know her so well?

Page bit her lip. The truth was, the wig made her head itch and sweat. She couldn't stand the sight of the thing, but she knew that the wedding pictures would be prettier if she wore it. But glimpsing her best friend, she couldn't lie. "No and no."

April tossed the offending item on the sofa. "Good. Because I don't like it, either." She stepped forward and placed her hands on either side of Page's face. "This is the woman I want to see years from now. If nothing else, we can pull the pictures out and remember what it was like and how far we've come."

"You don't have to be nice and say that to me."

"Since when have I ever sugarcoated my words to you?" April smiled. "Now let's get going before I'm late to my own wedding rehearsal."

She guessed she'd been told. Ruby winked at Page and followed April out of the house. Page paused and looked at the wig. She knew she should insist on wearing it, but a part of her was grateful that she wouldn't have to. Stopping to glance in the mirror by the front door, she nodded at herself.

"Kosinski, let's go!" April called from outside.

Page grabbed her purse and walked out, locking the door behind her.

The rehearsal and subsequent dinner were at the banquet hall where April and Zach would be married the following afternoon. At April's insistence, Page had sat through most of the rehearsal. She hadn't wanted her to wear herself out before the big day. Sherri winked at her from the front of the room, where they had placed an arbor lit with twinkling white lights, and waved at her with the makeshift bouquet in her hands.

Ruby sat next to Page with wide eyes. “I’ve never seen something like this.”

“A wedding rehearsal?”

“A wedding.”

Page put an arm around Ruby. “Wait until you see this place tomorrow. It’ll be even louder and more chaotic.”

Sherri, temporarily relieved from her bridesmaid’s duties, took a seat next to Ruby. “Not as chaotic as a wedding in my family. Which is the reason Dez and I got hitched at a justice of the peace. I wanted to get married as quickly as possible, and I was still too sick to handle a big event. Best decision I ever made. Just don’t tell my mother that. She’s still smarting over my refusal to follow tradition.”

Page nodded. “You have to do what’s right for you.”

Ruby looked around the banquet hall at the tables that still needed to be decorated with tablecloths, floral centerpieces and candles. “Is this what’s right for April?”

"She wants to be surrounded by family and friends. So yes. Zach, too." Page grinned as they watched the couple lean in for a chaste kiss. "They're going to be happy with tomorrow."

An older woman approached the couple and spoke to them, then April turned to the group. "Dinner is about to be served, so go ahead and find a seat. Zach's grandma made us her famous ravioli and Sherri's mom her chicken enchiladas. There's plenty, so don't be shy about asking for more if you want."

Page whispered in Ruby's ear, "And trust me. You'll want to."

They stood and found their places next to each other at the long dinner table. Meanwhile, Dez walked up to Sherri and kissed her soundly. "You looked amazing up there," he told her.

"You're supposed to say that about the bride," Sherri quipped.

"I only have eyes for you."

Page wanted to sigh at how Dez looked at her friend. Would she ever find someone to look at her the same way? Or the way that April and Zach gazed at each other? Ruby nudged Page and pointed to the chair. "You need to sit, remember?"

"All right, all right. Who's taking care of who here anyways?" Page pretended to grouse, but smiled at Ruby.

At the head of the table, Zach stood and tapped a fork against his wineglass. "Before the dinner is brought out, I'd like to thank you all for being a part of our special day tomorrow." April stood, too, her eyes shining with tears, and put an arm around his waist. "Not everyone is lucky enough to be surrounded by family and friends, and April and I hope you know how much you all mean to the both of us."

"We love you." April kissed her fingertips and sent out air kisses to the group before tucking into Zach's shoulder.

He placed a hand on the back of her head and kissed her forehead. "Get all your tears out tonight because tomorrow will be all about smiles and kisses."

"These are tears of joy, mister, and you'd better get used to them. Because I plan on being happy every day for the rest of my life."

They shared a kiss and everyone clapped.

Page heard Ruby sigh. "What are you thinking, Ruby?"

"I want to have what they have someday, you know?"

"I do, too." She'd never had it with Chad, as much as she might have thought she'd been in love those first few years of marriage. But she hadn't shared with Chad anything like what she saw on display with her friends. He'd been a charmer, using flattery to get her to go along with what he wanted. He'd said words of love when it helped his cause. She'd kept her doubts about his true feelings for her to herself because she hadn't wanted to say something that might make him leave. She had wanted to be a part of a couple so much that she'd overlooked the flaws and cracks in the relationship. She'd really believed that if she pretended that everything was okay, it would be.

Next time, if there was one, she wanted to be true to herself and have a real marriage. She wasn't going to settle for less.

PAGE BROUGHT A mug of coffee into her bedroom and tapped April's foot with her other hand. "Hey, sleeping beauty. Time to get up. You're getting married today."

Her friend opened one eye, but burrowed deeper into the sheets. "Five more minutes."

"We have to be at the salon in twenty."

April sat upright and put a hand to her short blond hair, which stuck out at all angles. "Remind me what the stylist said. Wash or don't wash?"

"Don't wash." She handed April the coffee mug. "I appreciate you having them do Ruby's hair as well."

"It's not like they have to do anything to you, so why not? The girl deserves to have some glamour in her life." April had a sip of the hot brew and then patted the mattress. "She told me last night that she wants to wait for a love like mine and Zach's." Her face softened. "Isn't that the sweetest thing?"

Page sat next to April. "I bet we were all thinking that last night. I know I was."

"What about Mateo?"

"What about him? He's just my lawyer."

April waggled her eyebrows. "He'll be

there tonight. You should ask him to dance. We both know he's got the right moves."

Page groaned and covered her face. "Please stop matchmaking. He's made his feelings very clear."

"He was at the hospital every night when you were sick. A man who is just a lawyer doesn't do that." April looked at her over the rim of the mug. "You know you like him."

More than liked him. She was falling for him. "What I would like is for you to get dressed and out the door before we're late for our hair appointments." Page pushed April's legs off the side of the bed. "Sherri's meeting us there."

"Fine. I'll drop it." April set down her mug after taking another long sip. "For now."

At the salon, Sherri's Aunt Laurie took April first, while another stylist looked after Sherri and a third helped Ruby. Page stood behind the girl and asked her, "So what kind of look do you want to have?"

Ruby put a hand up to her hair and shrugged. "Don't know how much they're going to be able to do with this?"

Page's stylist, Ana, winked at the girl. "I have magic hands. Trust me. I'll make you look like a princess for the night."

Sherri put a hand to her short hair. "I'll take anything but spiky if you can. Seems like my hair grew back determined to stand straight up."

Grabbing a gossip magazine, Page had a seat in the empty chair next to where Ruby sat, a purple cape around her neck. She looked at her two friends and foster daughter as they prepared to get beautified. "I have to say that I'm glad I'm not a part of this torture."

April pointed a finger at her. "Don't think you're getting off that easy, my dear. I have something special planned for you."

"Like what? You're going to paste rhinestones and glitter to my bald head?" When April only smiled, Page felt her cheeks warm. "You're joking, right?"

"No glitter. But Laurie's daughter is going to come in a little later and do your makeup."

Page groaned. She didn't like much more than mascara and a swipe of lip balm. The natural look was more her style. "You really don't need to do that."

"She volunteered, so be nice."

"Aren't I always?"

Sherri snorted at that and it set April giggling as well. Page opened her mouth and stared at her friends. "I am nice when I want to be."

Ruby spoke up. "She's always been more than nice to me."

"Just wait until the first time you miss curfew, kid." April winked at Ruby. "She won't be so nice to you then."

Sherri closed her eyes as her stylist brushed out her wavy dark hair. "I thought my mom was never going to stop shouting at me when I did that."

"I know how moms can be," Ruby said quietly. "But Page is my friend, too."

Page shared a smile with the girl. "I think we'll be just fine."

Quiet settled among the women as hair got moussed, curled and teased.

Eventually, April said, "Before the day gets busier, I want to tell you each something. Page, we've been best friends for years. I hope you know how much your support and kindness has helped me through some of the darkest times of my life. Sherri, we've only known each other for a little over a year, but that doesn't make the bond we share any less. You two women are like sisters to me. I wouldn't want anyone else to stand up beside me on my wedding day."

Sherri dabbed at her eyes with the edge of her cape. "Don't get us crying. We have a long day ahead of us."

April reached out her hand toward the teenager. "And Ruby, I've gotten to know you pretty well these past couple weeks. I'm glad that you're a part of Page's life and mine."

Aunt Laurie stopped what she was doing with April's hair and passed around a box of tissues. "Good thing we didn't do makeup first."

Everyone laughed and cried.

MATEO ADJUSTED THE tie as he looked at his reflection in the rearview mirror of his car. He wondered why he was even attending this wedding. Sure, he knew April and had met Zach a couple of times, but there had to be a bigger reason, right?

He squinted. He knew the reason all right. Page hadn't left his mind all week. And if he really wanted to be honest, she'd been in his thoughts ever since he'd danced with her at that party last spring. If only she was well. More confident about her prognosis.

Sweat beaded on his brow, and he got out of the car and grabbed his suit coat from the back seat. Because the humidity in the air made everything feel thick, he trotted across the parking lot and entered the banquet hall. Inside, the coolness of the air-conditioning made him sigh with relief.

The large room where they were holding the reception was to his left, so he walked inside the dim room lit only by candles and tiny white lights. He saw Ruby and waved to her. She walked up to him and did a twirl in her purple dress. She wore what looked like a crown in her hair, which had been tamed into curls. "What do you think?"

What he thought was she looked huge and ready to have that baby any second. But he also knew he needed to be more sensitive than that. "You look great. How are you feeling?"

She made a face. "I wish everyone would stop asking me that. I'm fine." She placed a hand on her belly. "I'm not planning on having this kid anytime soon."

"Okay. Good."

She lingered with him as they walked through the banquet hall. Mateo found Dez at one of the empty tables near the front of the hall. They shook hands and patted each other on the back. Marcus mimicked Dez's motions. Mateo looked behind Dez. "Where's Sherri?"

"She's a bridesmaid. April said she wanted her whole Boob Squad standing up for her. And my warrior is eclipsing them all with how beautiful she looks. Wait 'til you see her."

Mateo raised an eyebrow. Boob Squad? He'd heard of stranger things, he guessed. "Sherri could wear a paper bag, and you'd brag about how good she looked."

Dez put a hand to his chest. "Can I help it that I'm a man in love?"

A twinge of longing struck Mateo's heart, but he knocked it away with a shake of his head. "You're just lucky enough that she finally opened her eyes to you."

"I'm not lucky. I'm blessed, Mateo."

Ruby sighed beside him. Admittedly, he knew how she felt.

Someone tapped on a glass. From the looks of it, he was April's dad. "If everyone would come closer to the arbor, the ceremony will be starting shortly."

Mateo escorted Ruby toward the ceremony spot. They found a place close to the arbor that was faintly glowing from the lit candles that decorated it.

Soft classical music started, and the side doors opened. Two men in tuxes walked out, followed by Zach and a woman who looked like his mother. When they reached the arbor, the main doors on the other side of the room opened. Breath caught in Mateo's throat as he saw Page walk toward the arbor. She wore a soft pink dress that floated around her. The bouquet she carried in her hands was pretty, but it couldn't compete with her beauty.

Ruby nudged him. "She looks good, doesn't she?"

"Magnificent." He could only breathe the word since his heart had seized in his chest. Was this the same woman who only days before had been fighting for her life? The one whom he'd tried denying any feelings for?

Behind Page, Sherri came forward followed by April, who was flanked by her parents. Zach put a hand to his chest and smiled widely. April's parents ushered their daughter toward her eager-looking groom. Each parent kissed the bride on the cheek before taking their places with the rest of the guests in the circle around the arbor. April handed her bouquet to Page and put her hands in Zach's. Stepping forward from the circle, a priest began the ceremony.

Mateo recalled the man's usual words about love and cherishing for the couple's benefit, but all he had room in his head for was the vision of Page. He kept his eyes on her even as she watched the bride and groom. She sniffled at one point and grinned when Sherri nudged her despite the tears in her own eyes. When the priest mentioned couples in the crowd to repeat the vows along with the bride and groom, Page's attention landed on him and he couldn't look away or pretend that he'd been doing anything but staring at her.

After the priest solemnized the union, Zach and April shared a kiss. Mateo wondered what it would be like to kiss Page. Ruby sniffed beside him, and he handed her his handkerchief. But he still couldn't keep his eyes off Page.

The lights in the hall brightened as the priest announced the new Mr. and Mrs. Harrison and everyone clapped. A DJ started music playing, and the guests found their assigned seats at the tables. Ruby handed the handkerchief back to Mateo. "Thanks. I didn't think people really cried at weddings. I thought that was just in the movies or on TV."

He tucked the handkerchief back in his coat pocket. "They're tears of joy."

"That's what April called them earlier, but I didn't quite understand it, until now. I'm crying because it made me so happy."

They found their table and he took a seat between Ruby and Dez. "She looked great up there, didn't she?" he said.

Dez grinned at him. "I told you my wife was earlier."

"I meant Page."

Dez turned his head to look at him. “Changing your mind about her?”

“I can think she’s beautiful without wanting to date her.”

Dez laughed and smacked him on the back. “You keep believing that and we’ll see where you two are in a month.”

PAGE FINISHED THE obligatory maid-of-honor dance with the best man, and gave her apologies to Dalvin. She needed to sit. The physical and emotional toll of the day had already caught up with her, and she needed not only to sit, but to also get some fresh air. She took the stairs slowly up to a second-floor balcony that overlooked the busy avenue the hall was located on. She leaned on the railing and watched as cars passed below her, and part of her wondered where they were going in such a hurry at the end of a beautiful summer night.

The door behind her opened, and she turned to find Mateo stepping outside to join her. “Needed some air?”

She gave a nod. “It was getting a little close in there.”

“Are you okay? You look flushed.”

She breathed shallowly, but nodded and put a hand up to keep him at a distance. "I just need to rest."

He left the balcony momentarily and brought out a folding chair and set it up behind her. She lowered herself into it. "Thank you. I haven't been taking it as easy today as I probably should."

He put a hand to her forehead and then her cheek. "You're warm, but that's probably from dancing and being inside."

"You don't have to take care of me."

"Funny. Because I figured someone needed to."

"I'm an adult, fully able to take care of myself. I don't need you or anyone else."

"Really? I'm not sure you've been doing such a great job of it lately."

She could feel her temper rising, the flush spreading out from her chest, down her arms to her fingertips. Her anger gave her the energy to stand and stare into his eyes. "What do you want?"

"Nothing."

She narrowed her eyes at him. "If you didn't want anything, then why did you follow me out here?"

When he started to protest, she cocked her head to the side. Finally, he shrugged. "Okay, so I did have a reason for coming out here." He paused, but then said, "There's no easy way to say this, but I found Ruby's dad."

It felt as if the bottom of her stomach had fallen into the strappy sandals she wore. "You're sure it's him?"

He nodded.

She had to sit down again. "Oh."

"I haven't approached him yet, obviously. I figured I'd set up a meeting with all of us. You. Ruby. Her father. And myself." He leaned against the railing. "We'll make it some place that's neutral. Like a coffee shop or park or something."

She put a hand on her chest where an ache had formed at the idea of losing Ruby. "Right. Neutral. I can't believe you found him so soon."

"It's actually been a while."

"I know, but I thought I'd have more time with her." She looked up at him and hated that her eyes burned with tears.

He crouched down beside her. "She really got to you, huh?"

Page chuckled and wiped at her eyes. “Oh, like she didn’t get to you?”

He put his arm on her knee, then removed his hand. “Sorry.”

“It’s okay, Mateo. You can touch me. I won’t break.”

“You won’t break, but I might.” He looked into her eyes, and she could see a war going on behind them.

She decided to end the war for him and leaned forward to press her lips against his. At first, she could feel the hesitation in him. But then he put his hands up to her face and deepened the kiss. She let her eyes close and reveled in the taste of him. It was like sugar. Sweet and probably bad for her, but she was enjoying it while she could.

Then he backed away, and she almost fell out of the chair trying to keep her connection with him. She opened her eyes and found him looking out at the traffic. “Sorry,” he mumbled.

“I’m not.”

He turned to face her. “It’s not fair of me to kiss you when I know that I can’t be with you. Blame it on the wedding and all the romance in the air, but I just can’t do this.”

"Why not?"

"You know why." He took a few steps farther from her, then turned back. "I'll contact you to let you know when we'll be meeting with Ruby's father."

She nodded and the next thing she knew she was alone on the balcony. Tilting her head back, she closed her eyes and let the loneliness that had started to build engulf her. She would lose Ruby…and Mateo. Probably had known it the whole time, but for a while, she'd let herself believe that it would all come true for her. That she would win just this once.

She opened her eyes and let her gaze fall to the cars passing below. If only she could get in one of them and drive far, far away.

CHAPTER NINE

PAGE WAS GOOD at using distractions to get over her pain. She had done it after her cancer diagnoses, and she could do it again after the disastrous kiss with Mateo. The disaster hadn't been the kiss itself. That had been perfection. His words and disappearance after had been the big fail.

She'd returned to the ballroom and asked a friend to drive her and Ruby home. Then she'd kissed April's cheek and wished her well before leaving. She'd spent the next few days letting Ruby take care of her and pretending that everything was okay, when the truth was that her heart hurt. She'd hoped that spending time with Mateo had changed his mind about her. Obviously, it hadn't meant anything.

Unfortunately, she couldn't use work to distract her since her oncologist wouldn't let her return to a shift for some time yet.

Dr. Frazier worried about her white-blood-cell count. Because of the chemo and the infection, her immunity was low. She could catch any germ that she'd come in contact with, and something minor could be fatal. She had to accept the realities of her situation.

She scrolled through the news on her laptop, but couldn't concentrate on anything in particular. Ruby had complained of being tired, so she was in her room napping. At least Ruby's activity kept her interested in what was going on. She knew she should tell her about Mateo finding her father, but he hadn't called to set up a time for them to meet yet. And Page wanted to keep Ruby with her for just a little longer. Selfish, she realized, but the teen had been a blessing.

Someone knocked on her front door, and by the time she reached it, the person on the other side of it was knocking continuously. "All right, all right. Who died?" She opened the door and was faced with her ex, Chad. She narrowed her eyes. "What do you want?"

He looked as if he hadn't slept in a week—his face was haggard, his clothes disheveled. His normal smug grin had been replaced with something that looked like panic. "I'm so glad you're home."

He didn't seek her out on a normal basis, so this visit was definitely unusual. "What's wrong?"

Chad grasped her arm. "You need to come with me. Nikki is in trouble." He pointed at his car in the driveway. "She's there. In the car. Please. Just look at her."

"Is she in labor?" It was way too soon. Doing the math quickly, Page guessed Nikki was only five months or so along.

He tugged her outside. "No, but there's something wrong."

She shook off his hand. "I'm a labor-and-delivery nurse, not an obstetrician."

"Please, Page. There's no one I'd trust more."

She noticed the fear shining in his eyes. "I can call Dr. Achatz if you want, but there's nothing I can do."

"She insists that she's fine, but I know there's something wrong. Please come with me."

The tone of his voice, pleading and fearful, convinced her to go with him.

Nikki frowned when Page opened the car door and crouched down. "What's going on, Nikki? Why are you breathing like that?"

Nikki, panting, glared at Chad. "I told you I didn't want to come here." She pulled her arm away when Page grasped her wrist to check her pulse.

Chad leaned in. "Nikki, give me a break. She knows what to do."

Despite Chad's insistence that she did, Page wasn't completely comfortable with his confidence in her. She had studied about pregnancy complications, and had seen and experienced quite a lot, but Nikki really needed a doctor. "Can you tell me what's happening?"

"I'm fine," she answered through clenched teeth. "Can we go now?"

Page backed up, unsure what to say or do next.

"Don't go." Chad turned to Nikki. "Either you tell her or I'll take you to the ER. I don't care if you think you're okay, babe, you're not."

Page wanted to tell him that that's what he should have done in the first place. Nikki gave a curt nod. "Fine. I've been having these dizzy spells for the past few days followed by headaches. But I figured it's just morning sickness or whatever." She put a hand on her belly. "Then when I met Chad for lunch today, I stood up, and it felt like something was ripping my insides. I can't seem to catch my breath."

Page glanced at Chad. "She needs to go to the emergency room. This could be serious."

"That's what I told her, but she won't go."

Nikki shuddered. "I'm afraid. Of what they'll tell me."

Page raised an eyebrow at this. She never thought she'd understand how this woman would feel. "I get it. I've had those moments, too. In the doctor's office. But listen, this is what's best not just for you, but for your baby. You have to be brave, you have no other choice, right?"

Nikki closed her eyes.

Page turned to Chad. "Her blood pressure might be spiking, which could lead to some big problems, like a placental rupture. If she doesn't get checked out, she could lose the baby." For the first time she looked at Nikki hard. “Go to the ER. That’s your best option.”

Chad raced around the car and got inside. “Thanks,” he called out and the car sped off.

During dinner, her cell phone chirped. She placed her plate on the coffee table and picked up her phone. Recognizing Chad’s number, she paused the movie she and Ruby were watching. “How is Nikki?”

“She’s going to be okay,” Chad replied. “You were right about the high blood pressure. Gestational hypertension, they said. If she hadn’t been seen by a doctor, we could have lost the baby. So thank you.”

“She’s not out of the woods yet. You need to monitor her diet and make sure she’s drinking enough water and getting some exercise. Take her for walks.” When he didn’t say anything, she checked the cellphone screen to make sure that they were still connected. Then she heard him crying. She’d never known him to cry. He’d always said tears were for wimps. “Chad, are you okay?”

“I’m so scared of losing them.”

Those whispered words made her heart

break. Sure, he might not have ended their marriage the right way, but she could understand his fear of losing so much. After all, he'd almost lost Page twice before the divorce. She stood and walked into the kitchen. "You need to take care of her, Chad. You need to be there for her."

"I know."

"You can't expect her to do all this on her own. She needs you."

He sniffled and gave a soft cough. "I know. Please forgive me, Page, when I couldn't be there for you like you needed me to be. I didn't know how to handle it. I was immature and a jerk, and I'm sorry."

"It's in the past." She glanced out into the living room, where she saw Ruby watching her from the sofa. "Listen, I need to go."

"Thank you again, Page. I couldn't have convinced Nikki to get checked out if it hadn't been for you."

"Don't forget what I said."

"I won't."

Page ended the call and returned to the living room. She put her plate back on her lap and restarted the movie. Ruby looked over at her. "Who was that?"

"The ex-husband. He wanted to thank me for helping him out."

"You two friends or something?"

Page wanted to laugh at the suggestion. She didn't think she could be friends with him because she didn't trust him anymore. But she could offer advice and at least he'd distracted her for a moment from how she'd messed things up with Mateo. She shook her head. "No, he's just Chad."

LULU OPENED THE front door to her apartment and waved Mateo inside. "You don't look so good, bro."

To be honest, he hadn't felt good since he'd left Page on the balcony at the wedding. He'd been so drawn to her that he'd gotten burned in her flame when she kissed him. His lips still felt as if he'd been scorched. He shook his head and handed his sister the bag of treats he'd brought her. "I wasn't sure if you had cravings yet."

Lulu stuck her head in the bag and squealed as she brought out a plastic tub of French macaroons he'd bought at a local bakery. "You remembered my obsession."

"How could I forget? You dragged me to

store after store looking for those cookies when you got a taste for them."

She reached up and kissed his cheek. "You're sweet."

He wasn't sure how sweet he was. He'd hurt a good woman like Page to protect his own heart. He glanced around the living room. "Where's Roberto? I thought we were going to a movie."

"He's working nights this month, so it's just you and me." She pointed to the sofa. "You sit. Do you want some iced tea or water or something?"

"I'm fine." He checked his watch. "We should get going if we want to get our tickets and some popcorn before the show starts."

She took a seat next to him. "Can we skip the movie?"

"Are you sure you're okay? Is there something wrong?"

He glanced at her still-flat belly, and she placed her hand there. "Besides horrible morning sickness that lasts all day, I'm fine. I'm just not in the mood to deal with crowds. I thought we could hang out here."

She was up to something. He'd bet on

it. When there was a knock on the door, she feigned surprise. “Now I wonder who that is?”

She went and opened the front door, revealing an attractive dark-haired young woman who handed her a casserole dish. “Thanks for dinner last night. The kids and I really enjoyed it.”

Lulu grabbed the woman’s arm and pulled her inside the apartment. “Ella, have I introduced you to my brother, Mateo?”

The woman gave him a smile. “Nice to meet you.”

He stepped forward and shook her hand, then dropped it just as quickly. “You, too.”

Both Ella and Mateo turned to look at Lulu, who smiled brightly. “I’ve been hoping to introduce you two. And look, fate stepped in.”

More like Lulu had arranged this little meeting. Ella glanced behind her. “I should get back to my place.”

“Ella lives on the floor above us.”

“Yep. I hate leaving my kids alone too long. Never know what I’ll return to.” She waved to Mateo. “Again, nice meeting you.

And thanks again, Lulu, for the casserole. I'd love the recipe, if you get a chance."

Lulu shut the door after Ella had left while Mateo returned to the sofa. He opened the container of macaroons and bit into a pink one that reminded him of the color of Page's bridesmaid dress at the wedding. He chewed and considered the cookie.

"You could have been a little nicer," his sister said, scolding him.

"I wasn't rude. I shook her hand and said it was nice to meet her." He shrugged. "You could have been more subtle. I don't need you to introduce me to single women. I'm all right as I am."

"You don't date."

"I don't want to."

He started to grab another macaroon, but Lulu snatched the plastic tub from his reach and took it into the kitchen. When she came back to the living room, she handed him a bowl of chips and set another smaller bowl of onion dip on the coffee table. "You brought those macaroons for me."

"I know, but I wanted to keep my mouth busy eating, rather than telling you something you don't want to hear." He brought a chip covered in dip to his mouth and chewed.

"I don't understand why you don't want to meet a nice woman." She flopped next to him and took a chip from the bowl. "You're a good-looking guy, I guess. You're successful and smart. You have a good heart, not to mention your own place and car. You're the whole package and have a lot to offer a woman."

"Not quite."

"What are you missing?"

He looked the chip over and dipped it into the dip before eating it. "I don't want to be involved with anyone. I have you and Dad." He smiled. "And soon, a niece or nephew. That's all I need."

"Okay, but what about wanting something more?"

The image of Page on the balcony popped into his mind, and he shook his head. "I can't."

"You won't. There's a difference." She put a hand on his knee. "I know that losing Mom was hard on you. It was hard on all of us, but that doesn't mean we can't love anyone else."

"It does for me." He rested his arms on his thighs and kept his gaze on the floor. "I couldn't go through that again. And Page is looking at me like—"

"Page is looking at you?"

"Forget it. It's not important."

"You seemed to be thinking about her there."

"She's not important because I can't let her be." He looked up at his little sister. "She has cancer like Mom."

"But she's not Mom. You don't know how things will turn out. No one does. Meanwhile, you could be happy with her. Maybe really happy."

He cocked his head to the side. "You think I don't know that? But I can't allow her to get close to me. It would kill me to lose her."

Lulu scooted closer to him and put an arm around his shoulders. She laid her head next to his. "I love you, older brother, but you're being ridiculous."

He snapped his head up and stared at her. "What?"

"You could leave the apartment tonight and get in an accident and die. No one is guaranteed tomorrow much less the next five minutes. That's harsh, but it's the truth." She reached out and grabbed his hand. "If there's anything to be learned from losing Mom, it's to hold on to what time we do have with those we love. Because trying to keep people at arm's length so you won't care about them isn't working, is it?"

"It was until Page."

His sister grinned. "So what are you going to do about it?"

"I'll be professional and treat her only as a client. Because no matter what you say, I can't let her in. I just can't."

WHEN MATEO ARRIVED at his office the next morning, he groaned at the sight of a scruffy bearded man waiting in front of his door. Any visit from Jack Novakowski, a friend and Detroit police detective in the narcotics division, wasn't likely to be a social one. He held out a cardboard cup of coffee from the shop down the street. Mateo unlocked the door and then accepted the cup. "A peace offering? This can't be good."

Jack took a seat and rested his feet on

top of Mateo's desk. He wore a T-shirt and cutoff denim shorts so perhaps it wouldn't be an official visit. He took a gulp of his coffee. "You haven't showed up to any of the softball games lately."

"I've been busy."

Jack crooked up an eyebrow at this. "Word on the street is that you're not as busy as you were when you were taking juvenile cases."

"On the street?" Mateo shook his head as he set his messenger bag and the coffee on his desk. "I'm expanding my caseload to include other family-law stuff. But then I'm sure you've heard that, too."

"Replacing, more like. You haven't taken a juvenile case in over three weeks."

"You're keeping track?"

Jack put his feet back on the floor and leaned forward. "I need your help on a case."

Mateo shook his head. "No."

"You haven't heard the details."

"If you're already bringing up juvenile law, then I know where this is headed." He could see the wheels twirling in Jack's brain, already trying to assess the best way to convince him.

"But you are the best."

"Was the best. I don't take those cases anymore."

"We all get discouraged and question our career choices from time to time, but that doesn't mean you just walk away."

"I have. So unless you know someone who is looking for a lawyer to help with a divorce or child-custody case…" He pointed to the door and sat to turn on his computer. "You know your way out."

"I was hoping I wouldn't have to bring out the big guns, but you've given me no choice." Jack stood and pulled out a photo of a child who didn't look directly into the camera, and Mateo recognized the background as the wall of a Detroit precinct. More specifically, the wall outside Jack's office. "She's seven and got roped into being a drug mule. No parents have come to claim her, but I know the gang the drugs are connected to. My guess is that no one will touch her now. Not unless they want to be incriminated."

Mateo tried to look away from the photo,

but he couldn't. "No prosecutor in Wayne County is going to charge her for a crime she's obviously too young to understand."

"You're right."

"So why are you here?"

"I don't want her to get lost in the foster-care system. And because she knows who gave her the drugs, she could be in danger of retaliation if they think she's talked. She's been given some hard breaks, and she needs someone to look out for her." Jack grabbed the photo and put it back in his pocket. "I was hoping that would be you."

"I'm not a miracle worker, Jack. You've seen what's happened to some of my clients in the juvenile system. I can't do this anymore. I won't."

"Fine." Jack picked up his coffee and walked to the office door. He turned back. "You remember what we once promised? That we would fight for those who couldn't. But I guess I'm doing that on my own now."

He slammed the door shut behind him.

Mateo put his head down and blinked several times before he allowed himself to start working. His coffee tasted bitter now and he set it aside.

The image of the child haunted him as he followed up on several cases. When his stomach growled to remind him that it was lunchtime, he saved the document he'd been working on and locked the computer screen. He stood and glanced at his cell phone. Before he could second-guess himself, he called Dez. "Hey, you free for lunch? My treat."

Dez laughed on the other end. "Uh-oh. Sounds like you're looking for a favor."

"You're right. I am. Lolly's?"

"Meet you there in five."

Mateo arrived first and got a booth for them. He fiddled with the menu though he already knew he was going to order the usual. The door to the diner opened and Dez entered. Despite the heat, Dez wore a suit and tie, the jacket concealing the weapon he had strapped at his side. Because of his job with Border Patrol, he often carried a gun. Dez took the seat on the other side of the table. "Since this is your treat, I'm ordering the works."

"Good. Because this is a huge favor."

After they ordered, Dez placed his palms

on the tabletop. "So let's hear it. Who do you want mentored?"

"I need something more than that this time. You and Sherri are still certified for foster-care placement." When Dez nodded, Mateo said, "There's a little girl who needs a safe place. I can't think of anywhere safer than your house right now." He paused because he didn't know what to do to get the girl out of his mind if this didn't work.

Dez stared at him. "Sherri put you up to this, didn't she?"

"She doesn't know a thing about this. You're the first person I'm telling."

Their burgers arrived, and they ate in silence for a while. Finally, Dez sighed. "Last week after having Ruby stay with us for a few nights, Sherri talked about adding to our family. A child who needs a family like ours. Maybe adopting a little girl this time. You're sure she didn't talk to you about this?"

"As one of my best friends, I assure you that she didn't say a word to me. And this is a temporary solution."

Dez pulled out his cell phone and pointed it at Mateo. "You've got to stop finding us kids who need us." But he said it with a smile before calling his wife.

Mateo pulled out his own phone and dialed Jack. It went straight through to voice mail. He waited for the beep. "I know of a family for the girl. Maybe we can set up a meeting between everyone. Call me back." He paused. "I'm not done trying to help kids, whatever you may think."

THE MALL PARKING lot was packed but April managed to find a spot and parked. She sighed and pointed at the ice-cream shop at the other end of where the Hope Center was located. "Rainbow sherbet sounds perfect right about now."

Page got out from the passenger side. "Nice try. Meeting first. We're late as it is."

She opened the back door for Ruby, who groaned as she scooted out of the car. "I feel like I've gained thirty pounds this last week."

Page helped Ruby to stand. "You and I need to start walking more. Exercise would be good for us both."

"It's too hot to walk." The girl waddled beside Page and April. "I'm with April. Ice cream would be better for me than going with you guys to another meeting."

Page linked arms with both stragglers. *"After."* She pulled them along and soon they were inside the cool meeting room. Sherri waved them over to where she'd saved them seats.

They took their places as the meeting began. The usual stories about setbacks and progress got shared. Some tears were shed, mixed with hearty laughter at April's story about getting lost in Rome during her honeymoon and having to depend on Zach's spotty Italian to get them found.

Then the director, Lynn, stood up. "Anyone else have something to share?"

Sherri raised her hand, shocking Page since she didn't usually say anything at these meetings. "Dez and I have decided to adopt another child. My cousin Mateo put us in touch with a little girl who needs us as much as we need her."

Lynn clapped her hands with the rest of the group. "That's wonderful news. And it brings me to our topic tonight. Finding the good in cancer."

Several groaned, Page included. She

couldn't find much good in what she'd gone through. She'd lost parts of her body, her marriage and the hopes of having a child. What could she point to that showed she'd gained anything from this horrible ordeal? Then her gaze slid to Sherri. Okay, so she'd gained a friend. A good friend, in fact. And their diagnoses had brought her and April even closer than they had been before.

Lynn continued. "We are so quick to point out what we've lost." She put a hand to her own chest. "I lost my mother to breast cancer as a young girl. What good could that be?"

Page agreed. She'd lost friends to cancer as well and it never became easier.

"But I am a strong, independent woman who learned early to rely on myself. Would I rather have had my mom growing up? Absolutely. Still, there are always rainbows after the rain, if you look for them." She pointed to Sherri. "Your cancer journey has brought another child into your family. And April, yours helped you learn to appreciate a man who is now your husband. Why don't we go around the circle and share something good that came from cancer?"

Page hated this part of the evening. Though she'd learned much when others shared what they were going through in their journeys, she dreaded when it was her turn to talk. Half the time, she passed.

Her turn was coming closer as she racked her brain. Something good. What good had she found in this, her third round of chemo and surgery? Had she found anything? Crud, it was her turn. She paused and glanced around at the other faces.

Sweat broke out on her forehead as a dozen pair of eyes stared at her. "Um…" She glanced at April. "Good friends?"

Sherri smirked. "Great friends, you mean." She blushed. "The love of a good man. He finally admitted his feelings for me when things got rough."

Once everyone in the group had shared, Lynn nodded. "I've discovered that I'm a leader who is full of compassion and strength. Let's hold on to those good things even on the days so bad that we can't get out of bed. If we can remember the good, the worst won't have such power over us."

April elbowed Page, who shook her head. It sounded very close to something her friend had been trying to tell her for a while now.

The meeting started to break up, as people congregated around the snack table. Suddenly, Lynn let out a piercing whistle. "I forgot to mention earlier. Our annual fundraising walk in October is coming up pretty quick. Make sure you sign up before you leave. We're looking for more walkers as well as family and friends. We want this to be a celebration, so the more the merrier."

Page narrowed her eyes at April. "You already signed me up, didn't you?"

April nodded. "And Zach. And his grandparents. My parents. Sherri signed up her whole family. It's going to be huge."

Ruby asked, "Can I sign up?"

Page put an arm around the girl. "It's the middle of October, right around the time you're due. We'll have to wait and see."

"I don't want you to be the only one without family," Ruby said.

For someone who didn't cry, Page had to blink back the moisture that had quickly formed at the corners of her eyes. She took a deep breath. "Then I'd love for you to walk with me."

They shared a smile and Page pulled Ruby closer for a long hug. Could she care about this girl any more?

CHAPTER TEN

MATEO HAD CALLED Thomas Burns, aka Ruby's dad, and set up a meeting. Page had promised Ruby that she'd go with her, so she looked in her closet for an appropriate outfit for meeting her foster daughter's father.

She pulled out a short-sleeved white lace blouse with a matching tank for underneath. The lace wasn't something she normally would wear, but this was the first time she'd be seeing Mateo since that horrible kiss. She wanted to look feminine, so the lace would work. She paired it with a pair of black capris and strappy sandals.

She checked the clock. He'd be here soon to pick up her and Ruby, so she played with the idea of wearing a head scarf. As hot and humid as it still was, she decided against it. She left her bedroom to find Ruby pacing the living room, holding her belly.

Page walked over and put her arms around the girl to keep her from moving. "It's okay to be nervous."

"What if he doesn't like me?"

"Why wouldn't he? You're great."

"But he don't know that."

Page smiled. "Then I'll tell him how fabulous you are." She squeezed the girl even tighter, knowing that their time together could be ending sooner than she would have liked. "It's going to be okay whatever happens."

"But what if you need someone to take care of you? I could stay a little longer to make sure that you're safe." Ruby's eyes pleaded with Page. "We can tell him that you need me more."

"I doubt you'll be going home with him tonight, so stop worrying. There's a whole court process we still have to go through." She heard a car door slam outside. "And Mateo is just the one to help us."

She walked to the front door and opened it before he had reached the porch. He stared up at her and she wished for the thousandth time she hadn't kissed him.

Okay, so that wasn't entirely true, because the kiss had been amazing. It had been better than any she'd shared with Chad. No, she'd enjoyed the kiss and wished they could share more. What she regretted was the way it had separated them. Even now, it felt like any closeness they'd once shared was now gone. And she could only blame herself and the need to kiss him.

He cleared his throat. "You look nice."

She gave a nod, trying not to let his words mean too much. She stepped back so that he could enter the house, but he said, "We should go."

She grabbed her purse and steered Ruby outside. The girl dragged her feet even as Page kept her arm around her and helped her toward the car. She opened the passenger door, but Ruby grabbed her hand. "Can you sit with me in the back?"

Page nodded and once she, too, was inside, Mateo started the car, and they began the journey to Ruby's new future.

"I told Thomas we'd meet him at Mario's, the Italian restaurant." He looked into the rearview mirror at them. "I hope pizza is okay."

Ruby turned her head to stare out the

window. Page knew that pizza was one of the girl's basic food groups, but nerves and anxiety had won their war over her. As Mateo pulled up in front of the pizzeria, Ruby placed both hands on her belly. Page asked, "Are you okay?"

"I'm not feeling so good," Ruby answered.

"It's probably just nerves. You'll be okay." Page unfastened her seat belt and took a deep breath. "No matter what, Ruby, I'm keeping in touch with you. We're friends, if nothing else, right?" Ruby nodded, but the sentiment didn't seem to reassure her. She bit her lip and took a moment before walking toward the entrance of the pizzeria. Page exited the car and told her, "Try not to worry."

Mateo gave his name to the hostess, who seated them in a large booth at the back. Obviously, Mr. Burns hadn't shown up yet. Ruby still rubbed her belly even as they sat and sipped on the ice water that the waiter had brought.

To cut the tension and perhaps to make their time go by faster, Mateo ordered a basket of breadsticks with tomato sauce to tide them over.

Page glanced at her watch. Ten minutes late. "He probably got stuck in traffic."

"Probably." But Mateo didn't look any more convinced of that than she was.

The warm breadsticks arrived and they dug into them, which allowed them to keep from voicing their fears that they had gotten stood up.

Twenty minutes late. Half of the breadsticks eaten. Ruby vibrated as if she would levitate off her seat.

After a half hour, Mateo got out his cell phone and stepped away from the booth to go outside to make a call. Page turned to Ruby. "Tummy still feeling bad?"

"Not since we ate."

Mateo returned. "We're going to go ahead and order dinner. Mr. Burns got out of work late and wanted to shower and change before coming over." He gave Page a look that told her there was more to that story, but he couldn't share it with Ruby sitting there.

Ruby saved them the trouble of finding an excuse to be alone by leaving to use the restroom. Page leaned across the table. "Quick. What aren't you saying?"

"He was going to bail on us, so I had to do some quick talking to get him to come. And there's still a fifty-fifty chance he won't show up." Mateo picked up a menu and flipped it open. "I'm thinking pepperoni."

"Doesn't he want to meet his daughter?"

"He's not convinced she is his. But I told him that meeting her wouldn't hurt him. In fact, it could clear up some questions he might have."

Page glanced toward the restrooms. "I don't know if Ruby should meet him then. Not until things are certain."

"It will be fine."

"I'm not so sure."

"No offense, Page, but you tend to look on the negative side of things. Let's try to stay positive until something happens."

He raised his menu higher, and she was tempted to make a face at him. But she remained mature and stood when Ruby came back to the table. "Everything okay, sweetie?" Page asked her.

"Sure. Just hungry."

Mateo nodded. “Me, too. I’m thinking pizza, salad and wings. Who’s with me?”

The waiter reappeared to take their order. Every time the door to the restaurant opened, the three of them turned to look and see if it was Mr. Burns.

They had just been served their food when a tall man with a somewhat familiar face came into the restaurant and swept the room with his eyes before his gaze fell on Ruby.

Mateo stood and approached the man before bringing him over to the table. Mateo slid into the booth next to the girl, and Mr. Burns took a seat on the end next to Mateo.

Ruby stared at the man, and he looked away. Mateo made a motion toward the girl. “This is Ruby Wilson. Her mother was Marcia.”

The man looked at her then. “Tom.”

Mateo handed an empty plate to him. “Why don’t we eat and get to know each other a little?”

They served themselves from the dishes on the table. Page picked at the salad, unable to eat with all the tension surrounding them. Finally, Ruby cleared her throat. "How did you meet my mom?"

Mr. Burns glanced at Mateo before turning to face her. "She was a good friend of my cousin Lydia. We met at her birthday party." He stuffed a slice of pizza into his mouth, probably to give him an excuse not to say more.

Page watched him as he ate. She had a feeling that the man had a lot to say, but he wasn't sharing many details. She also noticed that as much as Mr. Burns ate, Ruby had hardly touched a bite. She'd picked up her fork several times, but then had laid it back down. Page encouraged her to eat something.

Ruby looked again at her father. For it appeared that's who he really was. They shared the same short sloping nose, as well as similarly curved ears and long, slender fingers.

Ruby picked up her fork but only scooted a piece of lettuce across her plate. "My mom said you was a no-account drifter." Mr. Burns's head shot up at the comment, but Ruby continued, "She said you promised to take care of her, but you ran off when you found out I was coming. I know how that goes. Cuz Derek cut out as soon as I started showing."

Mr. Burns placed his napkin over his dinner plate. "Mr. Lopez said—"

"Why did you leave us? She needed you." Ruby's voice was soft, but insistent.

He stood abruptly. "I know what you think, kid, but I'm not your father. Your mama liked to run with the boys, and it could have been any one of us."

"You're a liar."

"It's why your grandmother kicked her out, isn't it?" He gestured over at Mateo. "I'm sorry, Mr. Lopez, but I'm not the man you're looking for." And he left the restaurant. Mateo rose and followed him outside.

Ruby dropped her head and started to cry. Page tried to put her arms around the girl, but she rebuffed the offer of comfort and folded into herself, rocking back and forth. "I'm sorry, Ruby. I didn't think it would go like this."

The girl continued crying as Mateo came back to them. "He drove off before I got a chance to ask him about a DNA test."

Ruby wailed and pushed her way out of

the booth and ran to the restroom. Page stared at Mateo. What were they supposed to do now?

THIS WASN'T THE PLAN. Mateo had assumed they would eat dinner, get to know each other a little better and then discuss the nitty-gritty details about custody in a calm, cool manner. He'd never figured that the man would deny Ruby within minutes of meeting her.

Mateo put his hands on his hips and surveyed the table still covered in food. "Maybe I should have met him on my own first. I didn't even consider this."

Page's eyes flared with anger. "Oh, really? You seriously thought we'd be having a happy family reunion right now? I told you I didn't want to see her get hurt."

"What do you want me to do? The judge gave us these instructions. We had to find her family."

"Well, it's obvious that he doesn't want to know Ruby. The fact that he was going to stand us up in the first place should have been a clue."

He stepped closer, desperate to try to reassure her. How could he have messed up so badly? Was he caught up in his feelings for Page?

"She's basically a kid herself, Mateo, and pregnant, and just lost her mother. She doesn't need this additional drama."

"I'm following court orders. The system isn't perfect, but it still works."

"Tell that to all your clients rotting in juvie." As soon as she said the words, she placed her hand over her mouth. "I'm going to go check on Ruby," she said as she brushed past him.

He hit his fist against the tabletop, and dishes rattled. He apologized to the family sitting in the booth next to theirs. When the waiter approached him, he asked for the bill as well as carryout boxes to take the food home. He doubted anyone would be interested in eating after this.

Page ran out of the restroom. "Did Ruby come this way?"

"No, I thought she was in there with you."

Page shook her head as tears started to fall. "No one's in there. She's gone."

Mateo pulled out his wallet and threw

down more than enough money to pay for their meal. He and Page hustled outside. "She couldn't have gotten far," he said. He pointed toward the street. "You check the stores next to the restaurant, and I'll check the alley. We'll meet back here in a few minutes."

They moved in different directions. He headed toward the alley to see if there was any sign of Ruby. He walked in one direction first, looking between the back entrances to see if he could locate her. He reached the end of the long alleyway, but there was no sign of her.

When he returned to his car, he spotted Page, who'd covered her face with her hands. Tears streaked her face when she looked up at him. "Where would she go?"

He put his arms around her and pulled her close, resting his head on top of hers. "I don't know. But we're going to need more people to help us look."

WITHIN THE HALF HOUR, the parking lot was full of friends and acquaintances ready to search for Ruby. Mateo had them pair off and sent the groups off in different directions. He stopped in front of Page. "We'll find her."

She could only hope he was right.

Page and April volunteered to stay at the parking lot just in case Ruby showed up there. After fifteen minutes, they leaned against Zach's silver sports car. Well, April leaned while Page paced. "I never even saw her leave the restaurant."

"She couldn't have gotten too far on foot. We'll find her."

Page crossed her arms over her chest and stopped for a moment. "I don't think she'd come back here." She started to pace again. "What if she goes to my place?"

"Dez and Mateo are checking there first."

Page's phone buzzed, and she answered it without looking to see who the caller was. "Ruby?"

"It's your mother."

Page closed her eyes. She had enough to worry about without her mother adding to her sad state of affairs. "Mom, I'm busy. I'll call you later."

"What's wrong?"

"Nothing. I'll call you."

Her mother sighed. "It's not the cancer, is it?"

"My foster daughter's run away."

"Remember the time you ran away? I was frantic until your friend's mother called to say you had turned up at their house." Her mother scoffed. "Now you know how I felt."

Page thought of the fight that had prompted her to leave her mother's house. She'd convinced herself that it would be better at her father's place, but he hadn't wanted her to live with him. She hadn't wanted to return to her mother, either, so she'd called her friend Jenny to come get her. "I have to go, Mom. Just in case she's trying to call me."

"Sucks to be a mother, doesn't it? I tried to warn you."

She hung up the phone before her mother could launch into her usual tirade. Her heart hurt for the pain Ruby was going through. What would it be like to lose a loving mother and then be denied by her absent father? Actually, Page had a good idea of how she felt.

Page knew what it was like to pin your

hopes on a dad who turned his back on you. She could remember her heart shredding as he blocked the door to his house and told her he couldn't have a daughter like her living with his perfect new family. She'd been replaced so easily, and it had made her chest ache. To this day, she hadn't spoken to her father since that day as a teenager.

She'd longed to find a place that she could fit in. It wasn't in either of her parents' homes, so she'd focused on her studies and found a job in a hospital, where people were happy to see her as she helped out wherever she could. She'd admired the nurses she'd met and had set her sights on a similar path. And then she'd married Chad, thinking she'd finally found her real family. But then he'd left her.

She could empathize with Ruby, had been in her shoes, longing for a family that didn't seem to exist. But where would the girl go? Where would she find peace? "I know where she is."

April immediately opened the door to Zach's car. "I'll drive."

Page shouted out directions as April steered them toward the public library.

Page was out of the car and running for the building before April had pulled the car to a full stop.

"Ruby!" Page hollered. She had to be here. She'd mentioned spending hours among the stacks before she had to go back out onto the streets when the library closed for the night. And this was where she had gone to her support-group meetings. It was a place of comfort and acceptance. It made sense that she'd come here. "Ruby!"

She ran up the concrete steps and wrenched open the door. She rushed through the second set of doors and scanned the large main room, hoping to catch sight of the teenager. Discouraged, she walked to the reference desk. "Have you seen a pregnant teenager? Her name is Ruby. I'm her friend. Her foster parent."

The librarian shook her head, and Page thanked her before scanning up and down the stacks looking for Ruby. She left the fiction section and ran into April by the reference texts. "Any sign? I was sure she'd be here."

She took the stairs to the second floor and checked the meeting rooms. No Ruby.

Page returned to the main floor and spotted April.

"We'll keep looking," her friend insisted.

"Okay. Let me visit the restroom before we go back to the pizzeria."

Page continued to look around as she made her way to the women's room, located at the rear of the library. When she pushed open the door, she gasped. Ruby sat on the floor in a puddle of blood. She looked up at Page. "Something's wrong," she said.

CHAPTER ELEVEN

RUBY WAS WEDGED in the front seat of Zach's sports car between the two women as April raced to the hospital. Page wiped the girl's sweaty forehead with wet paper towels she'd taken from the restroom. Realizing that people were still searching for Ruby, Page put the girl's hand on the wet towel on top of her forehead. "Hold this while I call Mateo to let him know we found you."

The girl nodded as Page removed her cell phone from her pocket and punched in his number. When he answered, she took a deep breath, hoping that her voice would stay calm. The last thing Ruby needed was to become more worried. "We found her."

"Thank goodness. Where was she?"

"Doesn't matter. We're heading to the hospital, so please thank everyone and send them home. I'll call later."

"Wait. Is something wrong?"

She glanced over at Ruby. "I'll text you."

"Okay. Take care of our girl."

She agreed and texted him what was happening with Ruby. She resumed wiping Ruby's brow with the paper towels. Ruby stared up at her. "Who was looking for me?"

"Mateo. Zach. Sherri. Dez. Sherri's parents. Zach's grandparents. Some of Mateo's friends." She tried to smile. "We were all worried about you."

"Why?"

"Because we care about you. You're special to us."

Ruby's face crumpled and she cried out, clutching her belly. Page looked straight ahead. "Can you drive any faster?"

"I'm trying." April's tight grip on the steering wheel was making her knuckles white. "Hang in there, Ruby," April encouraged.

Within minutes, they were at Detroit General and April hopped out and started barking orders to the ER staff, while Page eased Ruby out of the back seat and into a wheelchair.

Page followed behind Kenny, the ER

doctor on duty. “She’s fourteen and seven months pregnant. She’s had a lot of blood loss so we’ll need to get a transfusion started. She’s been complaining of pains in her belly all day, but I thought it was just nerves.”

He nodded as she gave him every detail she could remember. When they got to the trauma room, Ruby disappeared behind a curtain. Page stood on the other side until April walked up behind her and pushed her toward it. “Go. She needs you.”

She found the team working quickly to help Ruby. She skirted by them and came to stand near Ruby’s head. She pushed the damp hair out of the girl’s face and placed a kiss on her forehead. “It’s going to be okay.”

Ruby moaned. “It hurts so bad.”

“It will get better.”

“What about the baby?” Ruby asked.

Page met the doctor’s eyes. He gave a quick shake of his head, and she took a deep breath. It seemed that the baby wasn’t going to make it. She knew that it had likely been the case when she’d seen the amount of blood, but the confirmation made her heart break. The doctor's efforts had to now be focused on saving Ruby. "Let's worry about you first, okay?"

"But the baby… Your baby…"

She kissed the girl's forehead again, hoping that Ruby didn't see the tears in her eyes. "It's okay. But we're going to need you to push."

Ruby kept shaking her head and moaning. "No. It's too soon."

Page moved around so that she could look Ruby in the eye. "Listen to me. It's time. We need to work quickly and save you, okay?"

The girl started to cry. "Page, I can't."

"Yes, you can." She put her hand on Ruby's. "I'm not leaving you, okay? We'll do this together. Now take a deep breath like me." Ruby mimicked her, and they did it several more times.

The doctor moved the girl's feet into the stirrups and helped her scoot farther down the table. "Push now, Ruby." The girl grasped Page's hand in hers and shouted as she bore down. "Good. Push again," the doctor asked.

Page was desperate to help Ruby, but all

she had were words. "You're doing great, sweetie. Keep pushing."

Ruby grunted with effort, and Page pressed a kiss against her forehead. The doctor nodded. "Good. One more time."

Ruby laid back, and tears coursed down her cheeks. "I'm so sorry. It's too soon."

Page leaned over her and put a hand to her cheek. "There's nothing to be sorry for, okay? But you need to give one more good push."

"I can't."

"You have to. And I'm right here with you." Ruby did so, but silence filled the room when it should have held mewling cries of a newborn. Page bit her lip and struggled to keep her composure for Ruby's sake.

The doctor placed the baby into the nurse's care. Page helped Ruby lie back down as the staff hurried to clean her up. She kissed the girl's forehead. "You did real good."

Ruby tried to get back up on her elbows. "What about the baby? Why isn't he crying?"

Page let the tears she'd held back fall

down her cheeks. "The baby didn't make it, sweetie."

"I lost the baby?" She started to sob, and Page held her in her arms, rocking her back and forth.

After a few minutes, the room started to clear of staff, and the doctor approached them. "Would you like to see her?"

It had been a girl. Page looked at Ruby, who nodded. "Yes, please."

He brought over the tiny baby, wrapped in a pink blanket, and placed her in Ruby's arms. Ruby moved the blanket away from the baby's face. "She was beautiful."

Page smiled at the sweet, tiny face. "She looks like you."

"I guess she does." Ruby leaned forward and placed a kiss on the baby's lips. "She was too beautiful for this world, I guess. Do you want to hold her?"

Page wiped at the tears on her face and nodded. She accepted the tiny bundle that weighed a couple of pounds, if that. She caressed the small cheek and pressed a kiss on the baby's forehead, which sported a fine dusting of dark hair. She was perfect and so still. "Do you think we should name her?"

"She was going to be your baby. What do you think?"

Page couldn't think of anything at the moment. The grief that pierced her heart made thought impossible. This might have been her daughter. In mere seconds, she imagined the life of this baby. Infant, toddler, child, adult fully grown, having an amazing future. But she'd never taken a breath. Page sagged on the bed beside Ruby and put her head against the baby's body and wept.

MATEO ENTERED THE emergency room and searched for Page, but didn't see her. He did see April and ran toward her. "How is Ruby?"

"She's losing the baby."

He took a step back and looked up at the ceiling, praying silently for both Ruby and Page. "What about Page?"

"I'm sure she's devastated. She really wanted that baby."

"I know." He gave April a hug. "Zach's on his way."

"Thanks."

It was hard for him to believe this had happened. Everything seemed fine only minutes ago and now this. How would it affect them all, especially Ruby? It might take a long while to deal with how this would affect them all. Ruby had become a big part of their lives. They all loved her and would now grieve with her.

The doors to the ER opened, and Zach rushed to his wife. He pulled her into his arms and kissed her as she cried. Dez and Sherri held hands. Mateo glanced around the room. Everyone seemed to have someone but him.

He could have someone, though. He could be putting his arms around her and comforting her right that moment if he wasn't so scared to open his heart to her. He walked up to the ER receptionist. "Is there a way to get word to Page Kosinski?"

The woman looked warily up at him. "She's a bit busy right now."

"I know, but I want to make sure she understands she's not alone. That we're all here for her."

Page came from around the corner. "You can tell me yourself."

She looked horrible and beautiful at the same time. Tears had reddened her eyes and cheeks, and it seemed that she hadn't finished crying yet. He pulled her into his arms. "I'm sorry," he whispered into her ear. "How's Ruby?"

"She's…okay. They're going to keep her overnight, so I'm staying with her."

He continued to hold her, but her arms stayed at her sides. When he let her go, she didn't look at him. "I need to tell everyone."

"I can do that."

"No, it's all right. It feels like my responsibility." She walked into the waiting room. April and Sherri sped to her side. They all had their arms around each other, crying. He watched them for a moment, then got permission to see Ruby.

In a private room now, Ruby was lying on the hospital bed, holding a blanket to her chest and rocking back and forth. She looked up at him. "I'm sorry, Mateo."

What? He put a hand on her shoulder, wishing he could do more to ease her mind. "Why are you sorry?"

"I shouldn't have run out of the restaurant. I shouldn't have run away. Things might have turned out differently. I wouldn't have let Page down then."

He frowned, unsure of how to explain her error. "I'm sure Page doesn't see it like that at all. None of us do."

"Us?"

"The gang. Sherri, April and their husbands, the other nurses and staff here. People care about you, Ruby."

"Not my dad, though. I don't know whether to wish he was here or be glad he isn't." She wiped her eyes. "Do you need to do a DNA test, or something, to prove Thomas is my father?"

It seemed like years ago that they had been attempting to have dinner with Ruby's dad. "I don't think he'll pursue custody, remember? Which gives us a couple of different options."

"Like finding another relative who will take me?"

He nodded. "That's one. Permanent foster care here, or in Oklahoma, is another. And then there's Page." He took a few steps forward. "What do you want, Ruby?"

Tears rolled down her cheeks as she stared at her lap. "What I want doesn't seem to matter anymore."

"Yes, it does. And I'm here to make sure I help you with whatever it is."

He squeezed her shoulder as a nurse entered. "We're going to check your vitals again, Ruby. Then you should try to get some rest."

He stepped back, but kept his eyes on Ruby. "I'm really sorry, Ruby."

She seemed to have aged a decade since he'd seen her earlier that evening. "It's okay. You tried to find me a family."

"I wish things could have turned out differently."

Ruby nodded. "Me, too."

"But you're not alone, okay? You have us."

Ruby held out her arm for the nurse.

"I'll tell Page where you are," he said and left the room.

He stood for a few minutes, collecting his thoughts, his emotions running wild. How he wanted to be of comfort to Ruby and Page. *Page?* He returned to the waiting room.

Page sat in one of the chairs, surrounded by her friends. He took a step forward. "They've moved her to her room now. Three forty-two."

Page gave a sad grin. "The children's ward. Even though she's no longer a child."

Everyone started to give hugs and words of farewell. Eventually, Mateo stood alone with Page. "How are you doing?" he asked.

"I'm tired, and Ruby needs me." She started to walk way, but stopped suddenly and turned to him. "You called her 'our girl.'"

"I did?"

"When I called to tell you that we were on the way to the hospital, you said to take care of our girl."

He tried to recall. "I guess I did." He vaguely remembered that. But then he'd been so relieved she'd been found and then worried about her and the baby. "Ruby's certainly found a way into our hearts, hasn't she?"

Page nodded. "I can't imagine a life without her now."

She put her arms around herself, and tears fell down her cheeks. He rushed forward and pulled her into his arms again. This time, she hugged him back. "It was a girl. She was so tiny and so beautiful."

"I'm sorry."

"It's not fair."

"I know." He rubbed her back in slow circles. "None of this has been fair."

Page took a step back and wiped her face. "I can't see the future. What it all means."

"Let's focus on Ruby healing. The rest can wait. It's too soon for some of those questions."

He drew her to him once more and kissed her cheek. "Everything's going to be okay."

Again, she didn't put her arms around him, but the hurt radiating from her was almost too much. Then she took a step backward. "I have to get back to Ruby."

She left the waiting room, her head and shoulders hunched forward as if she couldn't stand straight with the weight on them.

SUN STREAMED INTO the hospital room when Page woke the next morning. She had fallen asleep in a chair beside Ruby's bed, putting a crick into her neck and shoulders.

She rolled her head from side to side as she rubbed her sore neck.

Ruby still slept. Once things had calmed down and they'd had a chance to discuss it, Page had made arrangements for the baby's body to be cremated. Ruby figured she would do something thoughtful with the ashes once she was healed. Healed physically, at least. Page wasn't sure how long the emotional pain would last.

Ignoring the ache in her own chest, she stood and approached Ruby's bed. She put the back of her hand against the girl's forehead. A little warm, but nothing to be worried about. The girl's eyes fluttered, and she opened them and looked up at Page. "You're here."

"I told you I wouldn't leave. How are you feeling?"

The girl shrugged. "Okay, I guess." She winced against the sun that shone through the window and held up a hand to block out its rays. "Can we pull the curtain?"

Page complied. She longed for darkness as well. A dark room and her bed, where she could pull the sheets over her head and forget the last twenty-four hours. "Dr. Achatz said you can come home today."

"What home?"

Page frowned. "Mine, of course. Unless you don't want to live with me anymore."

"I don't care." Ruby pulled the sheet over her shoulder and turned on to her side away from Page.

She tried not to take it personally given what they'd both been through the night before. The girl was allowed to hurt. Maybe she too wanted to pull the covers over her head and forget.

The door opened and an orderly dropped off a food tray. "Breakfast."

"No thanks," Ruby mumbled and burrowed farther under the blankets.

Page nodded her thanks to the orderly. She pushed the table away from the bed. "I don't blame you. The food here isn't bad, but then it's not that good, either."

"Can we not talk?"

"Sure." Page returned to the chair she'd slept in and closed her eyes. The image of the baby's perfect face floated before her. Tears burned her eyes and she opened them to find Ruby's shoulders heaving.

She crossed the room and got into bed beside the girl, pulling her into her arms. "It's okay, Ruby."

The girl wrapped her arms around Page's waist. "I didn't even want the baby, so why does it hurt so bad?"

Page ran a hand through Ruby's hair. "Because she was a part of you for seven months. And the loss of her life is still painful. It means something. She meant something."

"It's not fair."

"You're right. It's not."

Ruby tried to push herself to sit up, but she moaned and clutched her belly. "It hurts."

"I know."

"I'm afraid that you hate me."

Page sat stunned. "How can you say that? I love you more than you know."

"But it's my fault."

Page refused to believe that. "It wasn't meant to be. Sometimes there are no answers. No good ones, at least. And *no one* is to blame for that, okay?"

"And you still want me to live with you after all of this happened?"

"Of course, I do." Page looked Ruby in the eye. "Do you still want to stay with me?"

Ruby nodded and buried herself in Page's arms. They held each other until their tears had stopped. Then they cried some more.

LATER THAT MORNING, April opened the door of the hospital room, bringing a wheelchair with her. "Your chariot awaits, Ruby. Dr. Achatz signed the paperwork to get you out of here."

"Good. I'm ready to go." Ruby glanced at Page.

April held up a bag of clothes. "I brought you something clean to wear home."

Ruby took the bag and headed for the bathroom. "Thanks."

April turned to Page. "How are you doing this morning?"

Page shrugged. "Every time I think I don't have any more tears left, I start crying again." She glanced at the closed bathroom door. "Ruby keeps saying she feels like she's let me down, but I don't know how else to reassure her."

"What are you going to do?"

"Take Ruby home with me. Mateo said they'll probably do a DNA test on the father and Ruby. That could take some time. But he doesn't want her, even if the test proves what we already suspected."

"And then?"

"Mateo has a line on her maternal grandmother in Oklahoma. I'm not sure about that, either. It's the same story. Why wouldn't she have come forward before now if she cared anything for Ruby?"

"What do you want to happen, Page?"

That was the big question she'd been mulling over since last night. She'd been so afraid for Ruby that she hadn't thought about what would happen now. The girl still needed her, and Page didn't want her to leave just yet.

If ever.

She'd become this girl's champion in a world that wanted to reject her. It had felt good to do something for someone else. But it was more than that. She loved Ruby's sense of humor. Loved the way the girl would reach out to help someone else, including her. She reminded her of herself at that age, and Page wanted to give her a better world than what she'd been given. To show her that life could be good even when you had no one. She didn't want to let Ruby go, but she wasn't sure if things had changed for the girl. If Ruby wanted to leave her. Would being with Page only remind her of what she'd lost? What they'd both lost? Or would Ruby be able to find comfort with Page?

April nudged her.

Page looked up at her and shook her head, unsure of how to answer just yet. The bathroom door opened, and Ruby appeared in a sundress. She placed a hand on her still-rounded belly. "I still look…" Forlorn, she stared at Page. "I thought I would look…flatter."

Page walked over to her. "You will eventually. Day by day, things will get back to normal. Your body. Your grief. It's going to all be okay."

Ruby nodded, and April joined them, putting her arms around the both of them. "I don't know about anyone else, but I'm in the mood for ice cream."

Page narrowed her eyes at her. "Since when are you not in the mood for it?"

"When things are sad, I like ice cream, can't help it."

"And when things are happy?" Page asked.

April smiled. "I like ice cream even more then. But with whipped cream and sprinkles."

Page checked to make sure they had taken everything. She found the discharge papers on the bed and grabbed them. She knew the drill—plenty of fluids and rest. No heavy lifting. Follow up with the doctor in the next few days. She'd given those instructions to enough new mothers that she could repeat them verbatim. The fact that they were leaving without a baby tinged the moment with sorrow. Page took a deep breath. It's like she'd told Ruby. Day by day, it would get better.

MATEO LEFT ANOTHER voice mail on Page's cell phone. He wanted to know if she wanted to see him as much as he needed to see her. She'd been on his mind from the moment he'd left the hospital, and those thoughts hadn't let up since.

He was falling for her. And that was the one thing he couldn't do.

Since he couldn't get in touch with Page, he figured he'd do the next best thing. The search for Ruby's grandmother was a little more complicated since they didn't share the same last name. He'd been able to locate a copy of Ruby's mother's birth certificate to get the grandmother's name. He rechecked the website he'd been reading and copied information onto his yellow legal pad.

Unfortunately, Sheilah Samson seemed to have disappeared shortly after the birth of her daughter. No public records mentioned her. No weddings or births or deaths in Oklahoma. She might have moved to another state. Or country. Or maybe she hadn't done anything of note since 1971. He could hire a private investigator to see if they could dig deeper, but he wanted to do this himself.

It would be his way to make up for Thomas. If he could find the grandmother and if she wanted Ruby, then… Then what? He saw how Page acted around the girl. Protective. Nurturing. What if the grandmother took Ruby away from the one woman who really cared for her?

He rubbed his forehead, then turned off the computer. Moot point really, since he couldn't find the grandmother. Besides, he needed to know for sure what Page wanted. If she even knew that herself.

His phone rang, and he picked it up without checking caller ID, hoping it was Page returning his call. "Mateo Lopez."

"You've got to get him out of that jail." The woman on the other end of the phone started to cry. "Scotty is in the prison infirmary."

"What happened?"

"There was a fight, and he seemed to get caught in the middle. Got beat up before the guards could separate the inmates." She paused, sniffling. "Why can't you get him out of there? He's just a boy."

Even though Mateo knew that the boy's own actions had led him to that spot, Mateo also knew she was right. He was too young to be stuck with the adult jail population. "I've tried to appeal to the judge, but because of the overcrowding situation in the juvenile detention center, there's no room for him there."

"Do whatever you have to do to save my boy. Please, Mr. Lopez."

She ended the call. Mateo stared at his cell before placing it on his desk. She was right. He needed to do something.

PAGE SHUT THE door to Ruby's bedroom and tiptoed down the hall. Ruby was finally asleep. Rest would bring more healing than anything else would right now.

April looked up from the sofa as Page entered the living room. "How are you?" her friend asked.

"She's finally sleeping, so that's good."

April stood and approached her, put her hands on each side of Page's face. "I asked how you were."

"I'm fine." She sidestepped her friend and went to the love seat, pulling the crocheted afghan over her. "Want to watch a movie?"

"No, I want to talk about this."

"There's nothing to talk about." Page reached over and grabbed the remote control from the coffee table and turned on the television. “Are you hungry? We could order pizza.”

April blocked the TV. “Page, we need to talk about this. The last twenty-four hours have been pretty eventful.”

Page sighed and tried to change channels. “I don’t need to talk, okay? You can talk all you want, but I really don’t have anything to say.”

“Fine.” April came and sat on the coffee table so that her knees touched Page’s. “I’m sorry you lost the baby.”

“I didn’t…”

“Yes, in a sense, you lost the baby, too. Sure, it was Ruby’s body that went through the trauma, but your heart was as invested in that baby.” April leaned forward and touched Page’s hand. “You’re focusing all your energy on Ruby so that you can ignore the pain and grief inside yourself.”

“Ruby needs me to be strong.”

April threaded her fingers through Page’s. “She’s not here right now. It’s just you and me. It’s okay to show your feelings.”

Page took in a deep breath and stared at the ceiling. Hot tears burned her eyes as she shook her head. "I wish you could have seen her. She was perfect. And so beautiful."

"I know."

"And I only got to hold her for a few minutes."

April scooted closer and put her other hand on Page's shoulder. "There can be other babies."

"Maybe." Page couldn't stop the rage any longer. "Just once—just once, one time, I would like to win and get what I want."

"So, you've had a couple of setbacks—"

"Couple?" Page laughed and stood—she could hear the hysteria in her tone. She moved away from April. The pain seemed overwhelming, and she had to get a grip on it again. Otherwise, how would she survive? How would Ruby?

In the kitchen, she grabbed a glass from the cupboard next to the sink and turned on the faucet. Drank the whole glass of water in one go, then refilled it. She leaned against the counter, pressing the cool glass against her warm cheek.

April stood in the doorway, her arms

crossed over her chest. “Can I join this pity party or are you celebrating alone?”

“I think I deserve it. Don’t you?” She’d lost so much already, and now this? She had done nothing to bring all this upon herself, and yet it had happened. The estranged family. The divorce. The cancer. And now, Ruby losing the baby. “You’re the one who wanted to talk about this, remember? I wanted to bury it all.”

“Talk about it, yes. Not wallow in it.”

Page drank the water and put the glass in the sink. “Go home, April. I’m not good company right now.”

“No.”

“No?”

April spread her arms wide so that she filled the doorway. “You’re going to have to force me out. And frankly, I don’t think you can.”

Page shook her head at April’s antics. As she hung her head and let the tears fall, April was pulling her into her arms and rubbing her back. “It’s going to be okay, Page. I know it doesn’t feel like it right now, but things will turn out all right.”

Page clung to April. "I don't know what I'd do if I didn't have you as a friend."

"Let's hope you never have to find out." April waddled them over to the counter, grabbed a sheet of paper towel and handed it to Page. "You haven't done anything to deserve these bad breaks, but you don't need to dwell on them, either. Now wipe your tears. Pity party is over."

Page did as her friend ordered, and she took several deep breaths. "I wish I could believe like you. That good things are coming."

"And how do you know they're not?"

She wanted to hold on to the hope that better days were ahead, but she couldn't see that far. And she'd learned early to expect the worst. "I'll tell you what. When I'm finally happy, you'll be the first to know."

"Deal."

There was a knock on the front door, and April left to answer it. Page so wanted everything to be right, but still, happiness seemed to elude her.

WHEN HE HADN'T heard from Page, he drove to her house. He tried to hide his disappointment when April answered. “Did Page know you were coming over?” she asked.

“No. I’ve been calling her all day, but she hasn’t returned my calls. How is she?”

“Why don’t you come in and see for yourself?”

April opened the front door wider, and pointed toward the kitchen. He followed her direction and found Page standing at the kitchen sink, staring out at the backyard. “Hey, Page.”

She turned, and he could see the tracks of tears staining her pale cheeks. “I was supposed to call you back.”

He waved it off. “It’s okay. I understand.”

“Do you? Because I don’t.”

He held out the bouquet of flowers he’d bought in hopes of cheering her up. “Here. I thought you might like these.”

She took the blooms from him. “Thank you.” She pressed them to her nose and then set them aside. “Why did you call?”

“I wanted to see how you were doing.”

She half smiled. “Okay, I guess.”

“Do you need anything?” He was begging for a crumb from her. He’d go on any mission that she’d send him. Take any order from her if it made her feel better. Because he didn't know what else to do.

He took a few steps forward, but the pain on her face kept him from getting too close. He didn't do emotions well, especially grief. He'd floundered after his mother's death, had been unable to heal himself much less help his father and sister through their own loss. Despite being book-smart and knowing the law, he couldn't fathom the human heart and all its messy emotions. Instead, he brought up another topic. "I haven't found the grandmother."

Page nodded, but didn't say what she was thinking. Her face had formed a mask of indifference. She seemed to be waiting for him to continue.

"Do you want me to find her?" he asked finally.

"Ruby deserves to be with her family."

"What if she's already found it here?"

Page gave a sharp bark of laughter. "Meaning me?"

"The two of you have formed a strong bond. In light of everything, she's really flourished under your care. Don't you want her to live here with you? Be a part of your family?"

"It doesn't seem to matter what I want." She looked at him with those big eyes.

"So I'll keep searching."

"It's probably for the best."

He wasn't so sure of that. He figured the woman before him was the best option for Ruby, but if Page didn't know that, he couldn't force the issue. "Okay then."

He started to leave the kitchen, then turned back to face her. "You didn't deserve to lose the baby, but that doesn't mean you don't deserve to be happy, either."

He left her house. The cold woman in the kitchen was a Page he didn't know. And he wasn't sure he wanted to.

CHAPTER TWELVE

THE TECHNICIAN PRESSED a cotton ball to Page's arm and removed the needle. She slapped the label with her vital information on her tube of blood and added it to the basket, which had two others in it. "Dr. Frazier will have the results within a few days."

Page knew the drill. They'd test her blood to see if the chemotherapy was working. To test the level of cancer antigens in her body. All of this to determine how long she would remain in treatment.

Slipping off the stool, she patted it and pointed to Ruby. "Your turn."

The girl paled. "We really don't have to do this. It doesn't matter to me if he's my father or not. He doesn't want me."

"Stop your worrying. They don't take blood for this test."

Ruby narrowed her eyes as if she didn't believe Page, but sat on the stool and waited for the technician to verify her name and date of birth. The woman pulled out a long cotton swab. "Open your mouth."

Page smiled at Ruby's surprised expression. "I told you it wasn't a blood draw."

The technician scraped the sides of Ruby's mouth and put the swab in a glass tube and capped it. "We'll send the results to your lawyer. Probably by the end of the week or so."

Ruby got off the stool, and the two of them walked out of the lab and down the hall to the waiting room, where Mateo sat, typing on his laptop. He looked up and smiled at them. "All set?"

Mateo drove them home. Page seemed glued to her seat and she watched Ruby go inside the house. Mateo spoke first. "No matter what the outcome of the test is, there's no guarantee that she'll go with Thomas. He seems pretty clear that he won't take her."

"I know."

He sighed. "What do you want me to do, Page? I'm your lawyer, and I'm not even sure what you want. You love Ruby, but you don't want to fight for her?"

"It wouldn't be a fair fight, would it? Like

you said, I'm dying and no judge would allow an adoption."

"So we give up? Just like that? Where's the woman who would stand up for what she wanted?"

"She's gone. Maybe it was all just an act anyway. And as for giving up, why not? You have."

"We're not talking about me."

"Perhaps we should. You won't fight for what you want, just like me."

"You don't know what I want."

She turned to him, her eyes blazing. "You want a perfect world where good kids don't go to jail and mothers never die. How is that working out for you?"

"Stop."

She opened the car door, kicking it with her foot. "Before you go lecturing me about fighting for what *I* want, you'd better take a good look in the mirror because you gave up a long time ago."

She stalked up the steps to her front door and didn't look back.

THE DARKENED ROOM told Mateo that it wasn't yet dawn. He rolled over onto his back and stared at the ceiling. Sleeping had become more difficult as worries about Scotty mounted. The image of the kid's face haunted his dreams, and he tossed and turned most nights. He had pondered different ways to get Scotty out of the adult jail population since his mother had called. He'd contacted the local juvenile facilities to see if there had been an opening, but they were overcrowded with the inmates they already had. He'd been researching alternatives, but hadn't found any answers.

When it became evident that he wouldn't get any more rest, he threw off the sheets and sat up. He wiped his face with one hand, then turned to sit on the side of the bed. He had to do something about Scotty.

After showering and drinking two cups of coffee, he pulled out his laptop and pulled up the visitation schedule for the jail. Based on Scotty's last name, Mateo could see him that afternoon at one. So be it.

A little before one, Mateo joined the long line to check in with the police officer in charge of visitation at the Wayne County jail. He edged forward when the person in front of him got out of line and left the building. Reaching the front of the line, he gave his name, and Scotty's.

The officer didn't look up at him, but kept his gaze on the computer screen. "Reason for your visit?"

To ease his own conscience? Find a solution to a problem when there probably wasn't one? Knowing the officer wouldn't appreciate either response, he answered, "I'm his lawyer."

Since he'd discussed what happened with Scotty with both Greg and Jack, he'd been stewing over how he'd let down Scotty with his sentencing. He should have fought harder to get his sentence changed. Should have argued that a kid shouldn't be housed with adult inmates. Maybe it was too late to fix things, but he had to come up with something.

He waited in another line before being ushered into a large gray room with metal tables and chairs. Taking a seat close to the door where the inmates entered, he hoped that Scotty would agree to meet with him for the allotted half hour. The door opened, and several men came out, moving to tables where their visitors waited.

Mateo kept his eyes on the doorway and sighed when the tiny form of Scotty entered. Scowling, he fell into the chair opposite Mateo.

The kid's face had yellow and purple bruises mottling his complexion, and he held his arm bent at his elbow and close to his body. But the biggest change was that his attitude seemed rough, hardened even, and it had only been weeks. "How are you doing in here, Scotty?"

The kid narrowed his eyes. "Don't call me that. Makes me sound like a baby." He crossed his arms over his chest. "They call me Domino in here."

Great. The kid already had a street name. "Are you doing okay, though?"

The boy shrugged. An inmate nearby scooted his chair back, and Scotty shot up, sitting straight in the chair. The freaked-out look on his face melted something inside Mateo. Despite Scotty's posturing, he was still a boy. Still scared and surrounded by angry men who probably gave him a hard time when guards weren't around.

Mateo leaned in closer. "I'm sorry

I haven't been to visit you before this. I should have been by."

"No biggie."

"You don't deserve to be in here. I'll petition Judge Gorges to move you to juvie as soon as possible." He paused at the hopeful look in the boy's eyes. "I can't promise that it will work. And he may want something from you before the transfer comes through, but I'll do my best. You can't stay here."

Scotty nodded. "Does he still want those names?"

"Probably, but that ship might have sailed. I'll set up a meeting with the judge and see what I can do."

Scotty reached a hand across the table. A guard approached them and rapped his knuckles on the metal table. "No touching. You know the rules."

The kid put his hands back into his lap and kept his gaze lowered. "I don't want to stay in here. Tell him I'll do whatever he wants me to do, and I'll do it."

"And this will be the last time you're in this situation?"

He raised his eyes to Mateo and gave a nod. “I swear.”

“Okay.”

A guard announced the five-minute warning that the session was ending.

“Before I have to leave is there any message you want me to give to your mother?”

Scotty glanced around and then dropped his voice. “Tell her I’m sorry. I won’t do this again. Promise.”

Mateo tried to give the kid a smile. “I’ll get to work on this. In the meantime, you stay strong. I hope to see you out of here soon.”

A whistle sounded, and the inmates rose to their feet. Scotty joined the line to exit the room, turning to look at Mateo one last time before leaving.

Back in his car, Mateo pulled out his cell phone and checked his directory. It never hurt to have a judge on speed dial. He pressed Gorges’s name and waited for an answer on the other end. When he did pick up, Mateo didn’t let him speak. “Your Honor, my client, Scotty Rodriguez, needs to be moved from the Wayne County jail immediately. I’ll be filing the paperwork for his transfer this afternoon. The courts don't want to be blamed for a kid who's gotten beaten up living with the adult population. It doesn't make for a good story on the six o'clock news."

"Are you through, Mr. Lopez?"

Mateo took a deep breath. "I'm just getting started. Your Honor, the prison system is meant to rehabilitate, but the only thing Scotty Rodriguez is doing is trying to keep himself alive. Please, sir, we need to move him."

"You're right."

Mateo paused and held his phone tighter to his ear. "I'm sorry. Did you say that you agree with me?" He glanced at his dashboard clock. If he could meet with the judge in the next hour, he could hopefully have Scotty transferred by the weekend or Monday morning at the latest. "So you'll sign off on the transfer?"

"That's not the question—it never was, Mr. Rodriguez. You have a short memory. It's whether there's room for him in the juvenile detention facility." The judge paused, as if weighing the matter. "I've finished hearing cases for the day, but I'd be willing to meet with you to see what we can do."

Mateo started the car. "On my way."

He met Judge Gorges in his chambers at the county court building. "Thank you for meeting with me on Friday afternoon, Your Honor. I know you'd rather be going home than trying to resolve this situation."

Judge Gorges glanced at him. "It never sat right with me sending that boy to the adult population."

"Me, either." Mateo took a seat and removed papers from his messenger bag that he'd been carrying since hearing about the prison fight. "All I need is your signature on these, and he can get transferred."

The judge pulled the papers toward him. "The only issue is where do we place him now. There are no beds available in either of the juvenile facilities here." Gorges raised an eyebrow at him. "What do you propose instead?"

Mateo took a deep breath. He'd read an article a few days ago that had made a brief mention of a program for teenage boys in the prison system. After several calls, he'd finally gotten an answer that afternoon.

Hopefully, the judge would agree to the alternative Mateo had come up with. "I've contacted Captain Wallace with the juvenile boot-camp program out of Cafferty County, and they have a place for Scotty."

"Cafferty County? You realize that is out of my jurisdiction."

"I understand that, but the captain has gotten Judge Peterson from that county to sign off on the transfer if you will agree." Mateo leaned forward in the chair. "Your Honor, it shouldn't matter who has jurisdiction over a delinquent minor, but it's truly the best placement for Scotty Rodriguez. The boot-camp program has a lower recidivism rate compared to our own county's juvenile detention center, along with lower rates of violence among the people who are there. Scotty will be safer and come out stronger than when he went in."

Judge Gorges held up a hand. "I can tell you've done your homework." He pulled out a pen to sign his name at the bottom of the page. "I take it you've also discussed this with his mother?"

"She knows it's a possibility and is willing to travel farther to see her son if it means keeping him safe, Your Honor."

The judge handed back the sheets of paper that had just changed Scotty's life. "Thank you, counselor."

Mateo nodded and took the paperwork, clutching it to his chest. "Thank you, Your Honor."

With the papers safely stowed in his bag, Mateo started to leave the office when Judge Gorges called his name. Mateo turned. "It's good to see you in my jurisdiction again. I hope this means you're back to helping our kids."

Our kids. Mateo glanced at the carpet, wondering if he could really return to all that implied. Could he go back to putting his heart at risk of breaking when he took on juvenile criminal cases? The truth was that he didn't see how he could live with himself if he didn't keep trying. There would always be another child that needed him, and he hoped that he would always find a way to help. He squeezed his hand on the doorknob. "I don't think I really left. Just needed a break."

"We all do at some point. We can't be

effective at our jobs if we don't take a step back every once in a while." The judge rose, joining Mateo at the door. "You put yourself on the line to save one of your clients today. That's why you're good at what you do. Just don't let discouragement keep you away from your purpose. To find a way where there is none. Like you just did for Scotty."

"What if my purpose is to keep kids out of being in a situation like Scotty's in the first place?"

"And how do you propose to do that?"

Mateo mulled over the question. "Something like matching up kids with mentors in the community, but on a larger scale. What if I could get more kids involved in the community by getting sponsors for after-school programs? By giving these teens not only a safe haven for them to hang out, but also activities to keep them busy and help them prepare for their future?"

The judge was silent for a moment. "You're going to need a group of people to help you with that one. Have anyone in mind?"

Mateo nodded toward the judge. "You've

always said we need to be involved in the community we work in. Can I count on your support?"

The judge laughed. "I see what you did there. Sure. Count me in. And it wouldn't hurt to hit up Greg Novakowski. I'm sure he's got ideas to back you up."

Mateo thanked him and shook his hand. "I'll be calling you."

He reached over and opened the door for Mateo. "Have a good weekend."

ZACH PUSHED BACK from the dining room table and patted his belly. "I don't think I could eat another bite, Page."

She protested. "But I have pie for dessert."

April groaned. "Really? Don't you think you've fed us enough?"

"I made dinner to thank you both for everything you've done for me lately. And dessert is to make sure you know how much you both mean to me."

Page stood and started to collect the dirty dishes from the table, stacking them on top of each other, cutlery and all. Carefully carrying them to the kitchen, she placed them next to the kitchen sink and focused on the apple pie she'd bought from the bakery around the corner.

April had followed her and her friend took small plates from the cupboard and opened a drawer to grab forks. "I'm disappointed that Ruby didn't want to join us."

"I know. She said she was tired and didn't want to eat anything."

"How's she been doing?"

It had been a little more than a week since Ruby had lost the baby, and Page was worried. Grief still laid heavy in her heart that she hesitated about how best to help Ruby. "She spends most of her time in her room, listening to music and lying on her bed."

"That's not good for her. She needs to be surrounded by people who love and support her. Not stuck alone in her grief."

"I don't know how to get through to her. It's like she's closed herself off from me. She won't talk about what happened or what happens next." She leaned on the kitchen counter. "I'm not her mother, where I could maybe make it all better."

"But you are her friend. Her best friend and she needs you."

Page shook her head. "I don't think she wants to be here anymore. And can I blame her? I haven't exactly been a barrel of laughs lately myself."

"Ruby is looking to you to set the example of how to grieve."

Tears gathered in Page's eyes. "That's the thing. I don't know how to get over losing the baby."

"So don't."

That wasn't the response she'd expected from April. She figured her best friend would tell her to get past it so that Ruby could. That she had to fake being cheerful and happy. "You're supposed to tell me it's going to be okay."

"I didn't say it wouldn't be. But this loss isn't something you just get over, like it's a cold or something." April placed the plates and forks on the kitchen counter and took the pie from Page's hand. "It's okay to cry."

"I'm done crying."

April raised one eyebrow. "Are you sure about that? Because you look like you need to right now." She put her arms around Page and hugged her tightly. “Let it out, Page. You’ll feel better if you do.”

The tears gathered and fell on their own despite Page’s efforts to keep them inside. She returned April’s hug. “I really wanted her.”

“I know.”

“But it seems to be that I’m not meant to have any family.”

April dropped her arms at those words. “Excuse me? And what am I?”

“You’re a friend. A good one, but you’re not family.”

April took a step back and peered into Page’s eyes. “Who do you have listed as your emergency contact?”

“Well, you, but—”

“And who is the first person you call when something happens?”

“You are.”

April nodded. “And whose family do you spend the holidays with?”

Page gave a small smile. “Yours.”

“Right. I think all that entitles us to call each other family, don’t you? We weren’t born to the same parents, but it doesn’t take having the same blood to make us sisters.”

Page pulled April into another hug as Zach entered the room. He put his arms around them both. "What are we hugging about?"

"Page being my sister," April told him.

He nodded and tightened his hold on them both. "I guess that makes me your brother-in-law."

Page took a deep breath and let them go, then wiped her eyes. "Okay, enough of this. Let's have pie."

April picked up the plates and forks while Zach took the pie with him to the dining room. Page trailed after them, but glanced down the hallway to the bedrooms. "Give me one minute."

"Tell her that if she doesn't get in here, she won't get any pie." April winked at her as she started to slice into the dessert.

Page put her ear against the closed bedroom door, hoping she could hear something. Silence. She knocked softly, turned the doorknob and stepped into the dim room. Ruby was lying on the bed, the covers pulled up to her ears. "Hey, kid. April says if you don't join us, then you don't get any pie."

"Don't want any."

April was right. She couldn't leave the girl to grieve alone. Page walked into the room and took a seat on the edge of the bed. "Why don't you come out and be with us anyway?"

"No thanks."

She placed a hand on Ruby's hip and rubbed it. "It's time to get up."

Ruby peered at Page, shadows standing out under her eyes. "Why?"

"Why not?"

"I don't feel like it."

Page nodded. "I don't feel like it, either, but that's part of growing up."

"And I have to eat pie?"

"No, but you have to join the land of the living again."

Ruby closed her eyes. "I don't deserve to."

"Yes, you do. You deserve to grow up and become the amazing young woman I know you are. Because yes, life is mean and hard sometimes when we lose something or someone we love. But that doesn't mean we shut ourselves away. Or give up on ourselves." She gestured to her own body. "Do you think I deserved to get cancer three times?" The girl shook her head vigorously. "Is it okay that I lost the baby, too?"

"No."

"You're right. It's not okay, but I still get out of bed every day and live my life. Even though there are some days I'd rather just pull the covers over my head." She reached out and cupped the girl's face with one hand. "Strong women like us don't get the luxury of staying in bed."

"You think I'm strong?"

"You wouldn't have survived all that you have already if you weren't." Page stood and held her hand out. "Now, come on. Let's eat some sugar and fat and pretend we're okay for the next hour."

"And after that?"

"Then we'll pretend we're okay for the next hour after that. And then the next day. And the next week. And then one day, we won't be pretending."

Ruby swallowed, but nodded and swung her feet over the side of the bed. "Okay."

"Good girl."

They left the bedroom together and in the dining room, April smiled at them and held up an ice-cream scooper. “We needed ice cream on our pie. What do you say?”

Ruby looked over at Page. “It’s easier to pretend with ice cream.”

Page drew the girl into a fierce hug, then mouthed “thank you” over her shoulder to April.

They would be okay. Maybe not today, but like she’d told Ruby, one day they’d wake up and realize that they weren’t pretending anymore.

On Monday morning, Mateo opened an official-looking manila envelope in his office. DNA test results. Sure enough, the man who had denied Ruby was indeed her biological father. He fished his cell phone from his pocket and searched his history for Thomas’s phone number and found it.

“Yeah?” a voice answered.

“Mr. Burns, it’s Mateo Lopez. I was hoping we could meet to discuss Ruby.”

“Just you?”

“Just me.” They made plans to meet at Thomas’s house. Mateo grabbed his messenger bag and slid in the paperwork for custody as well as those to terminate his parental rights. He wasn't sure how the man would take the news and wanted to be prepared either way. He also didn't want to call Page until he knew for sure how this would turn out. He'd learned his lesson.

Following the directions on his GPS, he drove to a neighborhood in the southern part of Detroit. He parked in front of a house that looked as if it had recently been repainted and landscaped. He got out of the car and walked up to the front door. A woman answered Mateo's knock. "I'm here to see Thomas Burns."

"He's in the backyard." She pointed around the front of the house to the left.

Mateo gave a nod and found Thomas weeding a vegetable garden. "Mr. Burns? I got the DNA test results."

Thomas paused and threw a weed into a pile next to him. "Okay."

When the man didn't continue, Mateo said, "They prove that Ruby is your daughter."

Thomas continued to weed, throwing the unwanted plants aside. "I told you. I don't have no daughter. Don't want one."

Mateo paused before pulling the paperwork out of his bag. "You know, Ruby is an incredible young woman. She's smart. Loves books. Knows every musical. She's got a laugh that would—"

"Like I said, I don't want her."

Mateo stared at the man. Some people weren't meant to be parents. He knew that in his head, but his heart couldn't understand. If he could be a dad to such a girl, Mateo would be bragging about her to everyone he met. After all, Ruby had taken care of herself for months after she lost her mother. She reached out to help others when circumstances arose, not holding back a thing. But instead, this man was going to miss out on knowing his amazing daughter. He thrust the papers forward. "These are for you to sign away your parental rights and absolves you of all legal and financial responsibilities for Ruby Wilson. If you truly don't want your daughter, then at least give her the chance to be adopted by someone who does. I just need you to sign them and I'll file them in court."

Thomas didn't look at Mateo for a long time, so Mateo took a few steps back and tucked the papers under an ashtray on the picnic table, so they wouldn't blow away. "Goodbye, Mr. Burns."

At the first grocery store he spotted, Mateo parked and went in. The tinny piped-in music of the store quickly grated on his already frayed nerves. Mateo navigated the shopping cart down the snack aisle, looking for something to improve his mood. He stopped to pick up a bag of tortilla chips and heard a giggle. When he looked over, he saw his father standing close to a woman, smiling, with a goofy grin Mateo hadn't seen in years. He thought about approaching them, but after all, his father hadn't introduced him to this new girlfriend.

He put the bag of chips back and turned to escape the potential awkwardness when he heard his name. He turned and feigned surprise. "Dad, what are you doing here?"

His dad held up a red plastic shopping basket. "Getting some things for dinner. Dalia said she'd cook for me."

Mateo shifted his gaze to the woman. She was shorter and thinner than his mom had been. She had short dark curls that couldn't seem to be tamed by the headband that held them back from her forehead. Dalia put a hand in the crook of his dad's elbow. "Nice to meet you, Mateo. Your dad has told me a lot about you."

But he's said so little about you, Mateo thought, but didn't share aloud. Manners indicated that he should shake her hand, so he held it out to her. She glanced at it, but then rushed forward and embraced him instead. "Sorry, but I'm a hugger."

He found himself being crushed to her. Hoping to find help, he looked to his dad, who only grinned at him. "What can I say, son? She's a hugger."

Dalia let him go and looked into Mateo's empty cart. "Do you have plans for dinner? I can cook for the two Lopez men just as easily as for one."

"I don't think—"

"Good. I hope you like steak. Oh, I need to get sugar. Can't forget that."

She rushed off and Mateo glanced at his dad. "What just happened here?"

"Dalia doesn't take no for an answer, so I guess you're coming to dinner." His dad paused and rubbed his upper lip. "If you really don't want to, I can make your excuses, but I'd like you to get to know her."

"I'm not sure I'm ready for this."

"No offense, but I don't think you'll ever be ready to see me with anyone but your mom." He shifted his weight from one foot to the other. "Still, I'd like you to give Dalia a chance. She's sure to charm her way into your heart."

"Like she did into yours?"

His dad nodded and then turned when he heard Dalia calling his name. "My house. Seven o'clock. Maybe bring something for dessert." Then he smiled and left him to it.

Mateo stood, holding onto his cart. He knew he should go to dinner and at least get to know this woman better. She'd put a twinkle back into his dad's eyes, and for that alone Mateo was grateful. Fine, he'd go, but he wouldn't let this woman enchant him like she had his father.

He purchased a key lime pie from the bakery.

Hours later, he arrived at his dad's house ten minutes before seven. He sat for a moment and looked up at the place. How would it feel to see someone cooking in the kitchen that wasn't his mother? Could he watch as another woman used the dishes his parents had received as a wedding gift? He took a deep breath and got out of the car.

His dad met him at the front door, hustling outside before Mateo could get in. “Before you go in, I wanted to give you a heads-up. Dalia is feeling a little apprehensive about this dinner. So be nice and eat it, no matter what it looks like, okay?”

“I’m not going to be rude, Dad.”

“I know, I know, but…” He glanced behind him. “She can’t a hold a candle to your mother in the kitchen. She tries, bless her, but she doesn’t follow recipes and relies on her instincts.”

“It can’t be that bad.”

His dad shrugged and threw open the door. “Mateo’s here!”

Dalia peeked around the corner of the kitchen. “Good. I’m just putting the final flourish on the steaks. I thought we’d try them with my take on a hollandaise sauce.”

His dad said, “Dalia likes watching those cooking shows on cable.”

“Sure do. Ray, why don’t you pour us drinks and, Mateo, you can take a seat in the dining room.”

Dinner was interesting. That was the best

word for it. That and unexpected, much like Dalia herself. Mateo had a hard time trying to put a label on her since she seemed to be everything. She cooked—or tried to—gardened, painted and knitted. She had held several jobs, but never one career. She'd worked as a waitress, receptionist, shop clerk and briefly as a librarian and substitute teacher.

Mateo nibbled at the potatoes that had been covered in the same sweet sauce as the steak. While it didn't taste that great, it wouldn't kill him. He attempted another bite.

"The sauce didn't turn out like I thought it would." Dalia poked at her meal. "I figured that the combination of sweet and salty would take it over the top."

His dad smiled at her. "It was certainly imaginative."

Mateo set his fork beside his plate. "I brought dessert."

Dalia sighed. "Good, because I don't think I can eat any more of this." She glanced at both of their plates. "Unless you're still eating yours."

"No, I've had enough." Mateo collected

their plates from the table and followed her into the kitchen, where she started to slice the pie into large pieces. "Thank you for making dinner, Dalia."

"Or trying to." She gave him a wry grin as she placed a slice onto a plate. "I'm not the cook your mother was. Ray has been telling me stories about the meals she made."

"I'm sure he's not telling you to make you feel bad."

"That's the thing. I don't feel bad. I know I can't compete with her, so I try not to." She nodded as she handed two plates of pie to Mateo. "Maybe I should leave the cooking to your father. He's so much better at it than I am."

Mateo noticed how she put a hand on his father's arm as she took her seat. A wave of grief washed over him for a moment. How much he wanted it to be his mother sitting at the dining room table. Willing those thoughts away, he took a deep breath and stared at the pie. He poked at it with his fork.

"It's all right, son. I miss her, too."

Mateo raised his eyes to his father's, then

glanced at Dalia. “No offense to you. But I keep thinking that I’ll get over it. To miss Mom less. But it doesn’t change.”

“It will once you find something to hope for again.” He placed his hand over Dalia’s. “Meeting Dalia helped me wake up and realize that I want to appreciate what I have. I started looking forward to each day. I want that for you, son.”

His career had for so long been enough. Fulfilling. And while he was glad he’d sorted out that part of himself, he knew he was still missing something. In his core, he suspected he knew what it was and how she affected him. *Page.*

Dalia cocked her head to one side. “Isn’t there anything in your life that puts a smile on your face?”

Page’s image popped into his mind, and the corners of his mouth twitched. The woman might make him worry and fret, but she was never dull. She could light up a room just by walking in and turning those big eyes on him.

“That’s it.” Dalia smacked the table and turned to his father. “Did you see that glimmer there?”

Mateo shook his head. “She’s not an option.”

“And why not? Is she dating or married?” Dalia asked him.

Mateo returned his gaze to his pie. “She’s got cancer.”

Dalia rolled her eyes. “Is that all? I had cancer, too, but you don’t see your father running out the door.”

Mateo choked and gaped at his father, who merely shrugged. “Dalia’s a three-year cancer survivor,” his dad said. “But that doesn’t stop me from wanting to know her better. Cancer is something that she had, but it’s not her. So why are you letting it stop something with this woman?”

“But you could lose her.”

His dad nodded slowly. “I’ve said it before, but anything could happen in the next day or week or year that would take us away from each other. Why not enjoy what is right now rather than worrying about what could happen?”

“Just forget that death is waiting to snatch her away?”

Dalia gave a hoot of laughter. “Your son should have been a poet, not a lawyer. I choose to remember that life is also waiting to be experienced and cherished."

"You remind me of April," he told them. "She would be saying the same thing to me right now."

"So why not take a chance and believe it?" Dalia asked.

Mateo considered it as he took a bite of the pie and chewed it. If his father, who'd lost his wife to cancer, could take a chance on a cancer survivor, then why couldn't he? Being without Page hurt, while standing next to her made him feel whole and happy. Even if they were searching for Ruby or sitting in a hospital room, her presence made it better because they were doing it together. He put down his fork and stood. "I think I need to go see Page."

Dalia clapped her hands as his father stood and put a hand on his shoulder. "Go get her, son. Don't miss out on her because of your fear."

With a smile, Mateo raced out the door. He needed to tell Page that he wanted to take a chance on her if she was willing to do the same with him. That a future without her wasn't one he wanted to face. He wanted her to be a part of all his days.

He looked down at the speedometer and realized that he was speeding. He eased his foot off the accelerator since the last thing he wanted was to be stopped for speeding on his way to tell Page he loved her. *Love.* The word made him happy. No more fear. He stopped at a red light and drummed his fingers on the steering wheel, impatience making his body vibrate. Finally, the light was green and he eased the car forward.

Headlights heading toward him made him turn to look. The last thought in his mind was that he'd never get to see Page again.

CHAPTER THIRTEEN

THE SMELL OF something baking brought Page awake from her nap on the sofa. She hadn't meant to fall asleep, but her body had cried out for rest. She sat up and sniffed. Smelled like something chocolate, and her stomach agreed by grumbling. Pushing the blanket off her, she walked into the kitchen to find Ruby dancing along with the radio as she took cookies off the pan and put them on a cooling rack. "They smell fantastic."

Ruby quit moving and turned to Page. "I didn't wake you up with the radio, did I?"

Page shook her head and moved closer to the freshly baked chocolate-chip cookies. "There's at least two dozen cookies here. You've been busy."

"I figured we both needed something to cheer us up." She held a cookie out to Page.

"My mom and I used to bake when things got tough."

Page bit into the cookie and nodded. "These are fantastic."

Ruby smiled. "Old family recipe."

Family. How much she wanted that for not only herself, but also for this girl who had so much to offer. The thought made the cookie stick in her throat, and she coughed. Ruby walked over to her and pounded her on the back. "Water," Page croaked out.

Ruby got a glass and filled it with water and handed it to Page. "Are you okay?"

Page gulped the water. "Thanks. The cookie went down wrong."

A knock sounded on the front door. Page said, "I'll see who that is, and then maybe you and I can talk about something good over cookies." It was time for Page to go after what she wanted. And that was Ruby.

Page answered the knock at the door. Thomas Burns stood there with papers in his hands. He thrust them at her. "Your lawyer isn't answering his phone."

She took the papers and glanced at them. *Termination of parental rights.* "You don't want Ruby?" She looked at him hard.

"I can't raise her. And I won't." He hung his head and shook it. "Like I told him, I'm not her father. But you seem to care about her and are there for her." He took a step down off the porch.

Page took a step forward. "Wait!" She looked at the paperwork again. She was Ruby's foster mom. She loved the girl, was so grateful she had come into her life. "Thank you. I've wanted nothing more than Ruby since I met her."

"Then be good to her. She's all yours."

Hers. Had there ever been any question that she wouldn't be hers from the moment they'd met in the ER? Page would fight to keep her, no matter what any judge told her. Ruby was her daughter in every way. "I will." She watched him get into his car and leave. She returned to the kitchen, but it was empty. "Ruby?"

A light down at the end of the hallway drew her attention. She approached Ruby's bedroom and pushed open the door to find the girl packing clothes into a duffel bag. She looked up and paused for a moment before pulling more items from the closet.

"Going somewhere?" Page asked.

Ruby took a shirt off a hanger and started to fold it. “I heard what Thomas said. He doesn’t want me. So I guess it’s time for me to move on.”

“You’ve got to stop running off when things don’t go the way you planned them. Otherwise, you’re going to miss out on some pretty great opportunities.”

“Like what? Being shipped between foster homes? Or spending holidays with strangers?” Ruby shook her head. “No thanks.”

“How about living here and spending your holidays with me?” She held her breath as she watched Ruby stop folding clothes and focus on something on her bed. “What if we became a family? You and me? I’m not saying that I could ever replace your mom, but I’d love the chance to be your second mom. That is, if you want me.”

Unshed tears glimmered in Ruby’s eyes. “You mean that? Or are you just saying it because no one else wants me?”

“I’m saying it because it’s true. I’ve never wanted anything more in my life.”

They stared at each other until Ruby let out a sob and pushed herself into Page’s arms. “I wanted that, too, but I was afraid you wouldn’t want me back.”

Page kissed her on both cheeks. “I worried the same thing. Why would you want to be around a sick woman like me?”

“Because there’s no one else I’d rather call family,” Ruby replied.

They hugged for a long while. Finally, Page let out a sigh and kissed Ruby again. “Okay. Let’s get you unpacked. And we need to figure out some things.”

Ruby gave her a final squeeze, then let go and started to toss out the clothes she’d packed. “What things? We want to be together. End of story.”

“I wish it was as easy as that, kiddo. Thomas may have signed off on his parental rights, but the judge still wants us to find your grandmother. What if she wants you, too?”

Ruby opened a dresser drawer and placed a stack of T-shirts inside. “If that was the case, where was she when my mom needed help? No, she gave up on me before I was even born.” Page handed her a hanger. “Why would I want to live with her?”

“If you’re sure.”

"You're not getting rid of me." Ruby jokingly made a face at her. "You're stuck with me. Isn't that what you told me not that long ago?"

"I'm usually right." Page smiled and accepted another hanger. "Okay, so we still have to get you registered for school." When Ruby groaned, Page laughed. "And we need to come up with some rules. School comes first. I expect you to study hard and do your best. Curfew is at nine, unless you're out with me. And..." Page paused. "What other rules do parents have? I'm new to this."

Ruby giggled. "That's probably not something you want to admit." She folded the empty duffel bag and placed it back in her closet. She turned and regarded Page. "I'll agree to curfew at nine, but I should be allowed to stay up until eleven. I'm not a baby."

"Nine thirty on school nights."

"Ten."

Page gave a nod and held out her hand. "Done."

They shook on it, and Page took a seat on the edge of Ruby's bed. "You're probably not going to want to hear this, but we need to do more shopping." She glanced around the room. "We could paint in here. Get you a new bedspread. And you're going to need more clothes for school."

Ruby groaned and dropped on to the bed next to Page. "More shopping?"

"I know how you feel, but I'm in the mood to spoil you, okay?"

Page's cell phone buzzed, and she pulled it out of her jeans pocket. A glance at the screen told her it was Sherri. "Hey, girl. Guess who just agreed to become my daughter?"

"That's great, but this is an official call. It's about Mateo."

The sound of her official officer's voice made Page pause, and her stomach flipped. "What's wrong?"

"He's been in a bad car accident. Can you come up to the hospital?"

"Yes." She hung up and looked over at Ruby. "We have to go. Mateo needs us."

PAIN. RAW, ANGRY pain ripped through him as Mateo tried to sit up. Someone pushed him back onto the bed. "Don't rip out my handiwork, Mateo. Just relax and let me do my job."

April's voice.

"Where am I?"

"Detroit General."

Mateo's eyes opened, and he winced at the harsh overhead lights. "What happened?"

"A car tried to take you out, but you're too tough for that." She turned to a nurse and asked for more gauze. "Now please lie there and let me find where you're bleeding so I can save your life."

He closed his eyes, remembered seeing the headlights rushing toward him. Thought he'd never see Page again, never tell her that he wanted to be with her. That made him groan even more.

"I'll fix you. Don't worry."

"Page. Where is she?" He was staring at April now, who was leaning over his left side.

She grinned. "Found the bleeder. Sutures. She's on her way. Sherri called her."

"I need her."

"What you need is to let me get you sewn back together."

"No. Page...she's all I need." He tried to sit up, but moaned at the pain that kept him prone.

To a nurse, April said, "He's going to tear these out if we don't sedate him. Sorry, Mateo, but I need you to lie still. I need to reset your leg and you don't want to be awake for that."

"Not until I see Page."

"After."

A nurse pushed something from a syringe into his IV, and everything became fuzzy, then black.

PAGE RAN INTO the emergency room with Ruby beside her. She searched the waiting room and saw Sherri and Dez. Their heads were bowed and Page worried that the worst had happened. It couldn't be. She was the one dying, not Mateo. Sherri saw her and waved her over.

Sherri put her arms around her. "Thank goodness you're here."

"How is he?"

Dez replied, "Car broadsided him going sixty plus. The firefighters had to cut him out. He's alive, but it's bad. Crushed his leg."

Page brought a hand to her mouth to stifle the sob. “No.”

A slightly pregnant woman approached her and put a hand on her arm. “Hello again, Page? We met a while back. I’m Lulu, his sister.”

“I remember. Your brother, he’s my…um, lawyer. And friend. And…”

“You love him.”

Page nodded and wiped at the tears that couldn’t seem to stop. For someone who didn’t cry, she’d done enough of it lately to last forever. “I can’t lose him.”

Lulu wrapped her arms around her. An older version of Mateo joined them and put his hands on both of their shoulders. “My son is a fighter.”

They took seats, Ruby offering to get drinks while they waited for news. Page gave her a fistful of bills and refused the others’ offers to pay her back.

She couldn’t lose him. Not when she could see the rest of her life ready to start. She’d lick this cancer and be Ruby’s mom, and she hoped to be Mateo’s wife eventually. She’d apply for the midwife program and find herself happy by being everything she'd always wanted to be. It wasn't fair that just as she was about to get it all, everything would once again be snatched away from her. She wasn't going to accept defeat. Not this time.

April entered the waiting room, and Page rushed toward her, the rest of his family surrounding them for news. "How is he?"

Her friend gave a thin smile. "I was able to find where he was bleeding internally, but his left leg is broken. We're sending him up to surgery. He's not out of the woods, but he's closer to being okay than he was when he came in."

Page closed her eyes and stepped back as his family started to ask more questions. She turned and found Ruby standing there, her arms full of pop cans. "Mateo's going into surgery," she told her.

"Is he going to be okay?"

Page allowed herself a small smile. "I think so."

Ruby returned the smile. "Hey, what's he going to say about you becoming my mom? And don't even try it that you don't love him."

Page's smile widened. "He'll have to understand you and I come as a package deal. But I bet he loves you as much as I do."

"You love me?"

"From the moment you told me you didn't need anybody to take care of you. I knew I had to be the one who loved you."

Ruby grinned. "I love you, too, Page."

"I'll remind you of that when I ground you for the first time."

MATEO OPENED HIS eyes to find Page sitting in a chair next to his hospital bed. When she noticed he was awake, she stood and put a hand on his forehead. "How are you feeling?"

"Like a car hit me."

She smirked at the comment. "Funny." Glancing at the door, she said, "I should go get your family. We've been taking turns watching you sleep, and they're going to want to know that you're okay."

He put a hand on hers on the bed railing. "Not yet. There's some things I need to say to you first."

"There's things I need to tell you, too."

He stared at her, unsure of what those things were now that she was there with him. "You're so pretty." He wanted to groan. *That's what I came up with?* He closed his eyes. *Concentrate, Mateo.*

"I look like hell, Mateo. But thanks, I guess."

He opened his eyes. "I love you."

"What?" Her mouth fell open, and she gaped at him, then checked the liquid bags hanging from the IV stand. "What do they have you on?"

"It's not the drugs. It's me. I love you, Page."

"Why?"

The question took him aback. "Because you're strong. And funny. And smart. Despite the odds being against you, you don't give up. And you love Ruby even though she could be taken from you. I want you to love me that way."

Page shook her head. "You stupid, stupid man. What if you had died before I could tell you?"

"Tell me what?"

"That I love you, too, you fool." She leaned forward and kissed him on the lips. "I need you, but don't ever do this to me again."

He reached up and touched her cheek. "If you love me, you need to hold on to whatever time we have. Whether that's a week or a year or fifty years, I want to enjoy it all with you. Isn't that what you've been trying to tell me?"

"I still have cancer. And your mom…"

"The cancer is something you both had. But it never was and never will be either of you." He caressed her cheek. "I see all of you, Page, and I'm in love with what I see. You are all about love and finding the strength for another day. Cancer won't take that away from you."

"I want to be with you so much, but there's something you should know."

That didn't sound good. "Whatever it is, it won't change that I love you."

"It's Ruby. She and I are a package, so if you don't think you can step up and be a father to her—"

"She's a part of my life as much as she is yours. How could you think that it would be a deal breaker?"

Page smiled and leaned down to kiss him again, but Mateo heard the sound of someone clearing their throat. A nurse standing in the doorway with a portable blood-pressure machine said, "If you two are finished, maybe I can take Mateo's vitals."

Mateo reached up and pulled Page's face to his so that their foreheads touched. "I think we're just getting started."

THE NURSE CHECKED Mateo's vitals as Page stood back and watched. His numbers looked good. Blood pressure. Temperature. Heart rate. He was going to be okay.

But still, Page couldn't believe her ears. He loved her. *Her.* After waiting and hoping for so long, he'd admitted he loved her as much as she loved him. *Could this be happening?* "Pinch me."

He frowned at her. "Excuse me?"

"This seems to be too good to be true." She stepped forward and put a hand on his face. "I've dreamed of this moment, but I never thought it would happen."

"Oh, it's happening."

Page leaned in for a hug.

Lulu entered the room, followed by Mateo's dad. "Can we get in on that hug?"

"The more, the merrier." They nodded and opened space for them to join them.

April arrived. “Is there room for a couple more?”

They all laughed and opened the circle wider to include her and Ruby.

Sherri entered the room and sighed. “Somebody scoot over and let me in.”

The circle of arms opened, and the seven of them hugged each other, smiling into each other’s faces. Tears started to fall down Page’s cheeks.

She’d always wanted to be part of a couple, but looking around at these faces she realized she’d been shortchanging herself. What she had was a family. Feeling their arms around her now, she figured she’d found herself a terrific one.

It didn’t matter what happened after today. Never mind the cancer, never mind anything else. With a family like this, she’d never feel alone or unloved again.

Mateo kissed her cheek. “You’re the luckiest woman I know.”

“Me, too.” She looked at April, knowing it was the truth. “I think I’m ready to be happy.”

EPILOGUE

THE MID-OCTOBER Saturday sky threatened rain, but Page didn't care. It could pour buckets, and it wouldn't dim her smile. She was at the beginning of the annual 5K walk with the other cancer survivors, waving at the crowd, with April on one side of her and Sherri on the other. Dropping to check the laces on her sneakers, she took a moment to appreciate what they were about to do. This year's 5K fund-raiser promised to be the most successful, if the attendance was any indication.

When she'd checked in at the park entrance, she'd turned in her envelope with the pledge money. She'd hounded friends and colleagues until she'd raised almost eight thousand dollars. Multiply that by the number of people here, and Hope Center would be able to reach out to more cancer patients and their loved ones. There was even talk about opening a second satellite office on the west side of Detroit.

April stretched her arms up and out as she glanced at the sky. “It better not rain.”

Page replied, “It won’t. Hope Center needs every dollar we’re raising.”

“I’d give the money to them even if we don’t make the full five kilometers.” Sherri pulled one leg behind her back. “I’ve been taking the kids on walks for the last few weeks to prepare them for today.”

“How’s Nala fitting in with your family?” April asked.

“Good. She’s finally sleeping through the night without waking up screaming.” Sherri shuddered. “I can’t even imagine what happened to her before she came to live with us. Dez accuses me of spoiling her, but I can’t help it. There’s so much of her previous life that I’m trying to make up for.”

“And Marcus?”

“He’s her protector and won’t let anyone at school bother her.” A wistful smile graced her face. “If you had told me two years ago that I’d be married to Dez and the mother to two adopted kids, I’d have laughed in your face. This was definitely not the plan."

"Cancer has a way of changing that," April said, waving at Zach.

Lynn blew a whistle to quiet the crowd. "We're going to be starting the walk in a few minutes, but I wanted to thank all of you and your family and friends for making sure we exceeded last year's total." People clapped and whistled. "Okay, when the gun goes off, you survivors will start us out. Family and friends will meet you at the two-kilometer mark and will finish the course with you. We'll have our celebration at the end with prizes and draw the winner for the fifty-fifty raffle. Any questions?"

"Who raised the most money?" asked a voice from the back of the pack.

Lynn smiled. "I know I saw her here. Where are you hiding, Page?"

Page raised her hands and started jumping. "Yes!"

Lynn motioned to a woman, who shot off the starting gun. "Let's go!"

Page started walking quickly, mostly to keep up with Sherri, whose long legs were giving her an advantage. “Hey, it’s not a race.”

Sherri turned and smiled at her. “Sorry. I want to get to my family as soon as I can.”

April looped her arms through Sherri’s and Page’s. “Maybe we can take this first kilometer together.”

They walked silently along the cement path for a while. Page could hear birds chirping as well as the fallen leaves crunching under their feet. “April, who besides Zach is waiting for you at the next stop?”

April smiled. “My mom and dad. They couldn’t make it last year, so this is going to be amazing. And Zach’s grandparents. We tried to get Zach’s mom to join us this year, but she’s had a rough couple of days. Her doctor felt it would be better for her to sit this one out. What about you, Sherri?”

“Dez and the kids are here, of course. And my parents, brothers, sisters-in-law, nieces, nephews…” Sherri let out a chuckle. “When you ask the Lopezes to show up for one member, the entire family gets involved.”

Page leaned over to look at her. “Same for me with Mateo and his family. We’re officially telling them today." She fiddled with the diamond ring on her finger.

Sherri nudged April. "How's the weight of that engagement ring on your finger feeling?"

They laughed and Page's heart leaped. "Just fine, thank you very much."

"And what about Ruby?" April asked. "Has the adoption officially happened yet?"

"Judge Bond had been reluctant to agree, but after discovering that Ruby's grandmother had died years ago, and with her father giving up his parental rights, he okayed it. It'll be official in a couple of weeks. By the way, Ruby brought a couple friends with her today. She's really liking high school.

"You know, Sherri, what you said before about not picturing your life like it is now? I never realized how much I've gained because of cancer."

"Like Mateo?"

"Yes, but it's even more than that." She paused to take in the people and beauty around her. "No, I mean that I've learned to accept what *is* rather than regret what *isn't*."

"I feel the same way." Sherri picked up the pace.

April nudged them both. "The Boob Squad together again."

Page wrinkled her nose. "What about changing that name? What would you say to calling us Survivor Sisters instead?"

April bit her lip and glanced at Sherri. "I like it. You?"

Sherri agreed.

"Survivor Sisters," Page repeated, liking how it sounded on her lips. "I couldn't ask for two better women to be by my side through this journey."

The three of them clasped hands and continued walking. They made a turn in the path and could see their families and friends waiting for them in the distance, cheering them on.

Page stopped walking and the other two stopped with her. April frowned. "Are you okay, Page?"

"I'm happy. No more Nurse Doom and Gloom." She could feel the corners of her mouth twitch into a smile. "I love my life. I love Mateo and Ruby and the two of you."

April winked at Sherri. “Uh-oh. Here comes the waterworks.”

Page shook her head. “I do have some news that I haven’t shared with anyone yet.” She looked at the ground, then up at them. “Dr. Frazier called a couple days ago. My blood work shows the chemo is working. I’m beating this thing.”

“Yes!” April punched the air and then hugged her. “That’s wonderful news, Page. I knew you could do it.”

“I couldn’t have done it without the both of you.” She hugged Sherri next. “Thank you for standing with me.”

“Our pleasure.” April looked up at the group that waited to join them on this walk—they were all applauding and shouting their names. “What do you say we go and celebrate?”

Page nodded and put her hands around April’s waist. Sherri put her arm around Page’s waist, and the three women walked on together. Survivors bound by hope and determination.

* * * * *

Don't miss other romances in the Hope Center miniseries from acclaimed author Syndi Powell:

Afraid to Lose Her
Healing Hearts

Available at www.Harlequin.com today!